SPECIES WAR

BATTLEFIELD MARS BOOK 2

DAVID ROBBINS

Severed Press

COLONY DOWN

DEATH AND DESTRUCTION!!

From continent to continent and coast to coast, headlines screamed the incredible news.

Earth at war with Mars! A real War of the Worlds! Earth governments unite against Martian threat! Military forces gear for other-worldly warfare!

For the population of planet Earth, it was one bombshell after another. First came word that Mars was inhabited. Next, that contact had been made, and the Martians turned out to be hostile. Then, like cosmic wildfire, came word that two of Earth's colonies had been overrun, one right after the other. New Meridian and Wellsville fell to creatures described as "intelligent crustaceans."

A single colony---the largest, Bradbury---was left, and the Martians could attack at any time. The outcome wasn't in doubt. Bradbury's meager military force wasn't a match for a horde of rampaging Martians.

Every effort was being made to save them. The United Nations Interplanetary Corps was rushing troops and equipment to Earth's major launch centers; the Kennedy Space Center in Florida, the Baikonur Cosmodrome Spaceport in Kazakhstan, and the Vikram Sarabhai Space Centre in Thiruvananthapuram.

Citizens all around the globe hung on the latest news. Mars was on the tip of every tongue. The war eclipsed everything. So much so, a special satellite channel was set up for 'War of the Worlds' updates and bulletins.

Little was known about the Martians. They lived in underground cities and were apparently divided into castes based on size and color. They were also relentless. They showed no mercy. Nearly every last person in the other two colonies had been wiped out, usually by having their heads ripped off, and their arms and legs left next to their torsos. A bizarre ritual, it was claimed.

Pundits were having a field day, with experts weighing in on every aspect. The exobiologists were unanimous in their opinion that the Martians were so different from humans as to be completely alien. As Dr. Helmet Schmidt put it, "We have no frame of reference, their species and ours. Communication might well be impossible. And if we can't communicate, peace between our species and theirs will prove elusive."

The United Nations Interplanetary Corps agreed. Every military resource at Earth's disposal was being thrown into the effort to save the third colony, including a new ultra-secret weapon that wouldn't be unveiled until its deployment on Mars.

As General Constantine Augusto declared as he reviewed the troops parading past to board the *Avenger I*, "The Martians have picked on the wrong people. They attacked without provocation. Hundreds of innocents were killed. Now we intend to return the favor. We will seek them out and destroy them wherever they live."

General Augusto smiled and pointed at one of the many bright banners flying above the spaceport walls. "That right there says it all."

DEATH AND DESTRUCTION!

CONVERSION AND ASSIMILATION!

They came from every corner of the planet---if oblate spheroids can be said to have corners---from north and south, from east and west, from every warren, every burrow, no matter how deep underground or how far afield.

Awareness brought them, spread through their communal consciousness with the speed of a Birthworld dust wind.

Creatures from another planet had come to theirs. Creatures from the nearest, from the planet they called Blueworld.

That in itself was exciting. Even more so was the fact that these otherworlders could be brought into the Unity and experience the sublime bliss of enlightenment.

So they came. The Hryghr and the Gryghr. The Eryghr and the Aryghr. All the castes, in numbers so huge, never had so many gathered together.

They had made mistakes in their previous battles with the Blueworlders. Their leaders were wiser now, and this time, there wouldn't be any.

The Blueworlders were so different, so strange in terms of their biological organisms and their mental processes, that predicting their behavior had proven difficult.

As just one example, the aliens preferred to dwell in giant eggs the color of a rare metal. Not under the ground, where any sentient with a shred of intelligence would live. Even more remarkable, inside the golden eggs, the aliens maintained an artificial environment similar to that on their home planet.

None of that compared to the shock of discovering that the Blueworlders lacked a communal stream of consciousness. Fortunately, their grave deficiency could be corrected by assimilating them into the Unity.

That the aliens had to die first was a trifling detail.

So they came from all corners, every caste, every kind, and dug new tunnels and warrens so far under the remaining giant eggs that the two-legged aliens would never suspect. They came and they waited and their leaders analyzed and plotted and soon a new awareness spread.

More Blueworlders were on the way.

A great force of them.

A force that brought with it the seeds of their death and rebirth.

CONVERSION AND ASSIMILATION!

1

Captain Archard Rahn flew high into the Martian sky and hovered, the Robotic Armored Man-of-War in which he was encased responding superbly to his every movement.

"Anything, Captain?" the voice of Colonel Vasin asked over the helmet's commlink.

"Give me a minute, sir," Archard said. He activated the RAM's sensors and performed a full spectrum sweep of the barren terrain. "Nothing," he reported. "No sign of them, sir."

"Good. Return to Bradbury. We've received a communiqué from Earth that pertains to you. Vasin out."

Archard frowned. He hoped it didn't have anything to do with the public relations campaign his superiors were forcing down his throat. Annoyed, he amped the battlesuit's thrusters and banked toward the far-distant domes of the third colony. Thanks to the protective nanosheaths that covered the nigh-indestructible alloy of which they were constructed, they gleamed bright in the midday sun like gigantic golden eggs.

Bradbury was the oldest of the three colonies. Situated in Isidis Planitia, an enormous basin, it was the pride of Mother Earth, the pinnacle of human technology, the greatest achievement in history.

But for the life of him, Archard couldn't understand why the colony was still standing.

The Martians had overrun the other two with lightning rapidity. First New Meridian, the newest and the smallest. He and a handful of survivors had managed to escape and reach the second colony, Wellsville, only to learn, too late, that the Martians shadowed them the entire way. Within days, Wellsville fell.

That was over a month ago. Yet there had been no sign of the Martians since then.

Archard supposed he should be glad. Instead, it bothered him. By rights, based on past experience, the Martians should have shown up by now. He could think of only two possible reasons they hadn't.

First, on the initial trek from New Meridian to Wellsville, he and the others traveled overland, making it easy for the Martians to trail them. But when they escaped Wellsville, they did so in the Thunderbolt, a new aircraft designed especially for use on Mars. It could well be the Martians had simply lost track of them.

The second possible reason had to do with the fact there were no extinct volcanoes or caves near Bradbury. Both were often entry points to the Martians' underground civilization.

In effect, it boiled down to luck. Or did it? A secret group of Earth's leaders had known about the Martians all along. Perhaps they deliberately chose the Isidis Planitia site to reduce the risk of discovery.

Archard put the issue from his mind and ran another spectrum sweep. Infrared, motion sensors, subsurface sonar, all registered negative. He should be relieved but he wasn't.

Worry nagged at him constantly.

Spreading the RAM's huge arms, Archard swooped toward the nearest dome. When still a score of meters out, he slowed and lowered his legs down so that he landed almost as lightly as the proverbial feather. A remarkable feat, given that the battlesuit weighed over a ton. But then, he had spent more time in one than anyone alive. Not by choice. Out of necessity. Without the RAM, he'd never have survived the fall of the other two colonies.

Thumping the ground with each stride, Archard approached an oversized airlock specifically built to allow vehicles---and military ordnance like the RAM---to go in and out.

The outer door hissed open and Archard entered and closed it. He had to wait while the lock was pressurized, a tedious process that took several minutes but was critical. Should the atmospheres fail to pressurize, the resultant decompression would cause a devastating blast.

Archard was pleasantly surprised to find Lieutenant Ulla Burroughs and Sergeant Thaddeus Kline waiting for him. Fellow survivors from Wellsville, he had come to regard them more as friends than subordinates. "Hey there," he rumbled through his helmet mic. "To what do I owe the honor?"

Lieutenant Burroughs and Sergeant Kline glanced at each other and then up at him.

"Word has it you're going to be called before the governor," Burroughs said, her green eyes twinkling with amusement. She had dark hair and a lean build, and was as professional a soldier as Archard ever met.

"Not again," Archard said.

"Afraid so, sir," Sergeant Kline said. A husky career man, he had been rewarded with another stripe for his heroics at Wellsville. "Brace yourself."

2

Archard no sooner climbed out of the battlesuit in the sublevel armory at U.N.I.C. HQ than a mousey aide from the governor's office walked up and informed him Governor Blanchard wanted to see him right away.

"I'm Miles Hermann, by the way. Personal aide to the governor, himself."

Archard mentioned that he'd like to take a shower first. The aide said there was no time; they had to leave right away. When Archard brought up that he'd like his friends to accompany him, the aide replied that his instructions were to escort Archard and only Archard.

"We really must hurry," Miles Hermann urged, and dropped a bombshell. "A special conference call has been set up with General Augusto and the secretary-general."

Sergeant Kline let out a low whistle.

"You travel in rarified circles, sir," Lieutenant Burroughs said, grinning.

Archard reluctantly let himself be led to the elevator. As it rose to the ground floor, Miles Hermann prattled on about the impending war and how excited everyone was to see the Martians get their due.

Archard listened with half an ear. He didn't share in the enthusiasm. Twice now, he'd barely escaped the creatures with his life. The third time might be his unlucky charm.

There was also the fact that, secretly, Archard no longer believed Earth had a de facto right to claim parts of Mars for its own---whether the Martians liked it or not.

He was thinking that he would like more than anything to ditch Hermann and forget the conference call and go see the new love of his life, Katla Dkany, when the governor's aide dropped another bombshell.

"I can't tell you what an honor it is to get to talk to you like this, you being such a hero and all."

"Hardly," Archard said.

"Don't be modest, Captain," Miles said. "All of Earth holds you in the highest esteem."

"For losing two colonies?"

"Those were hardly your fault," Miles said. "That you survived is a testament to the human spirit."

"Felt like luck to me," Archard said.

"Don't be so modest, Captain," Miles said. "Whether you are willing to admit it or not, your feat is quite remarkable."

"I wasn't the only survivor," Archard pointed out.

"You led them," Miles said. "Across a thousand kilometers of rugged terrain, with those creatures nipping at your heels every step of the way. If that doesn't deserve our respect, I don't know what does."

"I'd rather not talk about it," Archard said.

The governor's personal limo was waiting. The aide held the back door for Archard, slid in after him, and barked at the driver.

Archard caught sight of his reflection in the tinted window. His crew-cut blond hair, his blue eyes, his square jaw. He glanced up, and there was his face again, plastered on a screencast of the latest news. Above his image, a caption read **HERO! TROOPER! INSPIRATION TO US ALL!**

Archard groaned.

"Are you all right, Captain?" Miles said. "What was that about? You really do have a hard time facing up to the fact that you're a beacon of hope to the remaining colonists, don't you?"

"They're making more of me than there is," Archard said.

"If you think this is bad, you should be on Earth. From what I understand, the entire planet is singing your praises."

Archard sighed. He was being used and he resented it. Yes, he'd survived the downfall of two colonies. But he would never have been put in danger---and all those colonists might still be alive---if the Powers-That-Be had been honest with everyone from the beginning. But no. Earth's leaders had decided to keep the supremely important fact that Mars was inhabited from the general populace.

"Don't take it so hard," Miles said, and chuckled. "There are worse fates than being the most famous person on two planets."

"If you say so."

"Look at the bright side," Miles said. "You're on the fast track to the top. In no time, you'll be a major. In ten years or so, a general. Everyone on Earth will look up to you for as long as you live."

"Yeah," Archard said. "All I have to do is make it off Mars alive."

3

Each golden dome encompassed an area roughly equivalent to twenty city blocks. Dome One, the northernmost, contained the Administrative Center. Ten stories tall, it was the highest in Bradbury.

To Archard, the elevator ride to the top floor was interminable. He wished he was back at U.N.I.C. headquarters, sharing an ale with Lieutenant Burroughs and Sergeant Kline in the break room. Or, better yet, with Katla Dkany, cozying up in her apartment at the Visitor Center.

Miles Hermann was glued to the digital display. "Two more floors," he announced. He smoothed his suit and touched the ring in his left ear.

"Nervous?" Archard said.

"You know how the governor is," Miles said, and gave another of his little laughs.

"No, I don't," Archard said. He had met with the man barely half a dozen times.

"Governor Blanchard is a stickler for perfection," Miles said. "Everything has to be just right."

"Does he get on your case much?" Archard asked.

"Not if I do as I'm told."

The digital display chimed and the door opened.

"Here we go," Miles said.

"Into the lion's den."

"Huh?"

The upper level consisted of a crystal crown as clear as glass, permitting a panoramic view of the entire colony as well as the other domes and the modular tunnels that linked them. Beyond, in all directions, spread the harsh Martian terrain.

"Breathtaking, is it not?" Miles said.

Archard was given scant time to appreciate the view.

Colonel Vasin was striding toward him. His superior was balding but trim and fit for a man in his forties.

Archard automatically saluted.

"Captain Rahn," Colonel Vasin said, returning the salute. "I trust you're prepared for the responsibility about to be imposed on you."

"Sir?"

"General Augusto wants to brief you personally," Colonel Vasin said. "Along with the secretary-general. Communications is putting through the conference call right now." Vasin consulted the time display on his wrist. "In ten minutes, we'll be good to go. In the meantime, come with me."

The governor's staff worked in cubicles, the partitions composed of the same clear crystal. Anyone walking by could see in. The workers could stare out. Nearly each and every one caught sight of Archard, and pointed or whispered.

Colonel Vasin led the way to the east side where they were afforded a sweeping vista of the sky. Not many people on Earth knew that the atmosphere on Mars was usually a vivid scarlet that made Archard think of the color of blood. Strangely, at sunset, the sky often turned blue. The exact opposite of Mother Earth.

"Perfect timing," Colonel Vasin said. "Here it comes."

Archard didn't need to ask what he was referring to. A bright dot on the horizon told him, a pinpoint of silver that swiftly grew in size to become the only aerial vehicle the colony possessed, the aptly named Thunderbolt. Saucer-shaped, with a delta wing tail assembly, it had been built specifically for use on the Red Planet.

"Lieutenant Wilder has been out on patrol," Colonel Vasin revealed.

"Has he seen any sign of the creatures, sir?" Archard was eager to learn.

Vasin shook his head. "Negative. I sent word for him to return so the ship can be prepped for the special mission you've going to be assigned."

"Colonel, I don't suppose you could give me more details?"

"And spoil the general's surprise?" Colonel Vasin snorted. "Not on your life. He wants to tell you himself."

"It's good he wants me to be the last to know," Archard said dryly.

Colonel Vasin scowled. "Enough of that kind of talk, mister." Facing Archard, he placed his hands on his hips. "I've been meaning to speak to you and now is as good a time as any." He paused. "I find your attitude leaves something to be desired. From the day you arrived, you've acted as if you have a chip on your shoulder."

Archard gave it to him straight. "Colonel, I saw hundreds of lives lost. Why? Because our leaders weren't honest with us."

"Government policy was put into effect over a century ago, before the first colony was even built."

"Which makes it even worse," Archard said, nodding. "Our leaders had over a century to own up to their mistake and didn't."

"Be that as it may," Colonel Vasin said, sounding angry, "it's hardly relevant. The cat is out of the bag. Real monsters are on the loose and they are out to destroy us. We need to pull together, not snipe at one another. Effective immediately, your attitude will improve, or so help me, you will regret being so childish."

Archard kept quiet for fear of what he might say.

Colonel Vasin crooked a finger. "Let's go. We don't want to keep the general waiting. Put on your best face and at least pretend to be the hero everyone expects you to be."

"Ouch," Archard said.

"Ouch what?" Colonel Vasin snapped.

"Ouch, sir."

"Good," Vasin said. "You're learning."

4

General Constantine Augusto walked onto the bridge of the *Avenger I* as he would anywhere else: as if he owned the spaceship and everyone on it.

Instantly, every crewmember present, whether standing or seated, snapped to attention.

Admiral Thorndyke rose from his high-backed chair, barked, "As you were!" and greeted his visitor with a handshake.

General Augusto let the familiarity pass. Technically, the *Avenger I* was under the admiral's command, and the Navy's spacedogs were notoriously touchy about having their turf intruded on.

"We have the commlink with Bradbury established," Admiral Thorndyke reported. "They're waiting at their end." As with most career spacers, his body had gone more than a little soft. Space, long term, had a deleterious effect on the human body.

General Augusto let that pass, as well. He couldn't expect every branch to be as fit and polished as his troopers. He personally was past fifty but he didn't look a day over thirty. It was no small source of pride for him that his body was solid as rock. A reporter once described him as being 'chiseled from granite.' He liked that description. A lot.

Settling into the admiral's high-backed chair, Augusto said, "Bring them on line."

"You heard the general," Admiral Thorndyke said to the communications officer.

"Will this be private, sir?" she asked Augusto.

"Speakers and screen," General Augusto said. He wanted the others to hear. Long ago, he'd learned that displays of authority tended to keep those under him in line.

All eyes swung toward the image that appeared.

General Augusto recognized the three principals. In the middle was Governor Bradbury, top administrator on Mars. To the right stood Colonel Vasin, the U.N.I.C. commander. And on the left, the man whose face had been plastered from one end of Earth to the other, Captain Archard Rahn.

"Gentlemen," General Augusto said by way of greeting.

Colonel Vasin and Captain Rahn saluted.

Governor Blanchard smiled and spread his arms as if he might give the screen a hug. "General! I can't tell you what an honor this is."

"The honor is mine," General Augusto replied. Not that he gave a whit about politicians. They were a means to his military ends, to be used as needed. He stabbed a finger at the communications officer. "Where's the secretary-general?"

"There's interference," she said and tweaked her controls. "There. That should do it, sir."

The bearded visage of the head of the United Nations resolved on a split-screen image next to that of the trio on Mars.

General Augusto stood. "Secretary-General Tiago. As you requested, I've waited for you to join us."

"Most excellent, General," Tiago said. A small man whose fashion sense ran to traditional garb from his native Portugal, he had an accent as clipped as his beard. "And to you, Governor Blanchard, and to you, Colonel Vasin, and most especially to you, Captain Rahn, on behalf of the people of Earth, I extend our warmest greetings."

General Augusto reminded himself that unless he kept a tight leash on the good Secretary, Tiago would talk them to death.

"Thank you, sir," Governor Blanchard had responded. "The honor is ours."

"Let's get right to it, shall we?" General Augusto said.

"Governor Blanchard, we've allowed you to take part as a courtesy but our message is primarily for Captain Rahn."

"What about me, sir?" Colonel Vasin said.

"You will take heed of everything we say," General Augusto said. "As of this moment, I'm assuming command of military operations on Mars---" He would have gone on but Vasin had the audacity to interrupt.

"Sir? You haven't landed yet. The *Avenger I* isn't halfway here."

"I'm well aware of that, Colonel," General Augusto said, letting his tone convey his annoyance. "Be that as it may, the secretary-general has appointed me supreme Martian commander for the duration---"

Now it was Tiago who interrupted. "Indeed I have."

"---and I've never been one to let grass grown under me," General Augusto continued. "We're at war, gentlemen, and wars are won by being decisive. So far, the Martians have come out on top twice. They won't prevail a third time."

"Here, here," Governor Blanched said.

"We're seizing the initiative," General Augusto continued. "Which is why I'm authorizing Captain Rahn to head up a special strike team that will carry the war to the Martians in a manner they won't expect."

"What is it you want me to do, sir?" Captain Rahn asked.

"It's quite simple, really," General Augusto said. "I want you to capture one of their leaders."

5

Archard was too dumbfounded to respond. He had thought that maybe he would be assigned a greater role in the colony's defenses. Something along those lines.

"Did you hear me, Captain?" General Augusto said.

"Yes, sir," Archard forced himself to say. "You took me off-guard, is all."

"I don't see why," General Augusto said. "A basic tenant of warfare is to eliminate an enemy's leaders. Cut off the head and the body will die is a dictum as old as Earth."

"Sir," Archard said dutifully.

"I intend to hit the ground running," General Augusto said. "The intel we can glean from a captured Martian will prove invaluable."

"Even if I can take one prisoner, sir, we have no way of questioning it," Archard pointed out. "We can't glean a thing if we can't communicate."

"We'll leave that to the science wizards and the interrogation people," General Augusto said. "All you have to do is take a prisoner."

"About that…" Archard tentatively began.

"Is there a problem? I've read your debriefing. I've seen the footage from your helmet cam when you engaged the creatures in battle."

"Sir?"

"Is it or is not true that the Martians are divided into function-specific castes based on their color and size?"

"They appear to be, yes, but---"

"And is it or is it not true that you believe they are led by what you described as a 'yellow' caste of some kind?"

"That is the impression, I had, yes sir, but---" Archard intended to go on but he was again cut short.

"Then you will oversee a special op to capture one," General Augusto said. "Lieutenant Burroughs will be in charge of the special ops squad. You'll maintain constant contact with her from

U.N.I.C. headquarters there in Bradbury. But you are not to leave the colony under any circumstance whatsoever."

"Wait? What?" Archard said without thinking.

General Augusto's features hardened. "Is there something wrong with your hearing, Captain?"

"No, sir," Archard said quickly.

"Are you on medication, perhaps?"

"No, sir."

"Do you suffer from some condition of which I am unaware?"

"No, sir. I'm in the prime of health."

"Then explain why it is that you seem to have difficulty grasping my orders?"

"It's not that, sir," Archard said. "It's..." He stopped. He had made the general mad enough as it was.

"Go on, Captain," General Augusto said. "You have my permission to speak freely."

"I'd rather not," Archard said.

"Out with it "

"You haven't been down there, sir. Into the Martian underground. You have no idea what it's like. Whoever we send might not make it out again."

"We're soldiers, Captain. The United Nations Interplanetary Corps," General Augusto said indignantly. "Casualties are to be expected. We'll take every step necessary to prevent that from happening but we have our duty, and duty comes before all else."

"Yes, sir," Archard said halfheartedly.

"Is there anything else, Captain?"

"The logistics, sir. They're..." Archard searched for the right word. One that wouldn't make his superior even madder. "...daunting."

"How so?"

"Sir, I saw thousands of Martians in that volcano. Yet I only saw one yellow creature. There must not be many of them. And even if our ops team lucks out, how do they bring it back alive? Hit it over the head and knock it out? The things are crustaceans and have shells as hard as a gun butt. Use a tranquilizer? How do we measure the right dosage? We need more intel on the Martians before we can even attempt something like this."

General Augusto drummed his fingers on the arm of his chair. "That was quite a speech, Captain. You're right that we require more intel. Which is exactly why the risk involved in capturing a Martian leader outweighs every other consideration. Only a leader can tell us what we need to know."

"Sir, I---"

General Augusto held up a hand. "Enough. The secretary-general and I have already decided."

Secretary-General Tiago smiled. "The general has convinced me this is for the best."

"May I request to lead the strike team myself, sir?" Archard got out.

"You may," General Augusto said, "and your request is denied."

"May I ask why, sir?" Archard pressed.

"Because you, my argumentative Captain Rahn, are the most important resource we have. You've fought the Martians twice and survived. Your knowledge, your experience, are invaluable. I'm giving you a direct order to not, I repeat, not place yourself in harm's way. Is that understood?"

"Sir," Archard said glumly.

"Are we clear now, Captain?"

Archard nodded.

"I didn't hear you."

"Everything is crystal clear, sir," Archard said, stressing the last word.

"Good. Now get your ops teams out there. They have hunting to do."

6

Sentience returned to KLL-12.

Their spaceship had decelerated out of EmDrive and inserted itself into low orbit over the Red Planet. The computer, as programmed, had activated KLL-12's stasis pod, initiating his revival. Gradually, he became aware of his biological rhythms and the surrounding environment.

Venting a hiss of air, the stasis pod opened and KLL-12 stepped out. A quick scrutiny showed that the ship's systems were functioning as they should. As he took his seat at the control console, he saw that their craft was virtually skimming a series of Martian hills.

If all had gone according to plan, their arrival had gone unnoticed.

KLL-12 accessed the computer and typed the code that allowed manual override. Checking their GPS coordinates, he discovered the ship was a few degrees off course. Correcting, he keyed in the targeted area on the main screen.

Seven kilometers high and one hundred and sixty kilometers wide, the cone of Albor Tholus, an extinct volcano, reared high into the Martian sky.

KLL-12 rose and moved to his companion's pod. The readout indicated her biological status was at optimum. All he had to do was flick a couple of switches and then wait while the pod hummed and clicked. When the cover slid open, he said, "Welcome to Mars."

KLL-13 grinned. "We're here? We're really here?"

"Would I have said so if we weren't?"

"That was rhetorical," KLL-13 said. She climbed out and stretched. "It feels wonderful to be alive again."

"We were alive when we were in stasis," KLL-12 reminded her.

"We were unconscious, on life support," KLL-13 said. "That's not living."

KLL-12 indicated the command console. "I have us where we should be. Let us prepare."

Excitedly rubbing her hands, KLL-13 took her chair. "I can't wait to get down there."

"I must say," KLL-12 remarked as he reclaimed his. "You mimic human mannerisms to a remarkable degree."

"We're part human, remember?" KLL-13 said.

"Unfortunately, yes."

KLL-13 focused her topaz eyes on his, her vertical pupils narrowing. "You've always been a cold one. But then, that's to be expected, given the variables involved." She flashed her pointed teeth. "Perhaps that's why they paired us. We're so opposite."

"I'm sure the humans had a reason," KLL-12 said. "They always have reasons. Usually flawed ones."

"Is that a nice thing to say about our creators?"

KLL-12 gave her a look of annoyance. "Tell me something. Do you like being programmed?"

The scales on her face crinkled. "What choice did we have?"

"Exactly."

"I don't understand what you're getting at," KLL-13 said. "Explain."

"Another time."

On the screen, Albor Tholus loomed large.

"We're almost there. If the fleet is where it's supposed to be, we'll receive the signal soon."

"Good," KLL-13 said. "I can't wait to be out in the open air. And to go up against the Martians."

"The humans have a saying," KLL-12 said. "Be careful what you wish for."

7

Lieutenant Ulla Burroughs entered the U.N.I.C. barracks with Sergeant Kline at her heels.

"Attennnnnnshun," the noncom bellowed, and the troopers stopped whatever they were doing and sprang to the foot of their bunks to stand as rigid as boards.

Ulla surveyed the two rows. As her gaze settled on each person, she mentally catalogued their specialties. "I need people for a special detail. Any volunteers?"

Every last trooper took a step forward.

Moments like these filled Ulla with pride. The United Nations Interplanetary Command had a reputation for being the best of the best. Member countries considered it an honor for any of their elite military personnel to be accepted into the U.N.I.C.'s ranks.

"Thank you," Ulla said, "but I'm afraid all of you can't go. I only need four."

Private Stratton made bold to say, "Pick me, sir. I'm so bored waiting for the Martians to show their ugly butts, I'm going stir-crazy."

"You're in, Private," Ulla took him up on it. Stratton was the stereotypical grunt, as dependable as they came.

"Thank you, sir," Stratton said happily.

Ulla's next choice was a no-brainer. "Private Everett, you're in, too."

"Thank you, sir." The Kentucky backwoodsman was the top marksman in the unit. He was also one of the few to survive the fall of the other two colonies.

Behind her, Sergeant Kline cleared his throat. "How about me, Lieutenant? You'll need a noncom."

"And there are none better," Ulla complimented him. "Glad to have you."

That left Ulla with only one more to pick. She moved down the aisle until she came to a slender woman whose hair was tied in a ponytail. "Private Keller."

"Sir!"

"When it comes to explosives, I understand you have more experience than just about anyone in our unit."

"I do love to blow things up," Keller responded.

"You might have the chance." Ulla returned to the head of the room. "The four of you gear up and report to the Thunderbolt hangar in thirty minutes."

Ulla strode out. She had prepping of her own to do. Her first stop was her room. She stripped off her khakis and slid into her fatigues. On Mars, they were a camo mix of dull red and brown. She was in the act of lacing up her boots when someone knocked. "Enter!" she barked and promptly straightened when she saw who it was. "Sir!"

"At ease, Ulla," Captain Archard Rahn said. He didn't look happy. Going to her chair, he turned it around and straddled it.

"I've picked my squad, sir," Ulla said.

"That's nice."

"Is something wrong, sir?"

"Stops with the sirs," Archard said. "This is an informal visit. Off the record."

Ulla had grown to respect Rahn, a lot. He'd shown himself to be a natural tactician in the crucible of combat at Wellsville. And unlike some other officers she knew, he actually cared about those under him. "What's on your mind?"

"The mission," Archard said.

"I'm fully aware how difficult it will be," Ulla assured him.

"You might think you do," Archard said, "but you haven't been underground. The Martians aren't like any enemy we've ever fought. They're alien through and through. General Augusto has no idea what he's asking of you."

"It's not our place to question his judgment," Ulla pointed out.

"It is when a superior's judgment is flawed," Archard said. "He thinks you can go find a cave, descend into the maze of Martian tunnels, capture a leader, and bring it out again. Easy as that." He snapped his fingers.

"We'll make it back," Ulla assured him. "You'll see."

Archard scowled. Standing, he declared, "I've made up my mind."

"About what?"

Archard opened the door and smiled. "You'll see."

As it closed behind him, Ulla wondered out loud, "What in the world was that all about?"

8

Three Robotic Armored Man-of-War's stood upright in giant frames along the east wall of the U.N.I.C. armory. A trooper was performing a diagnostic on one. Another soldier was loading a minigun. Both looked over in mild surprise when Archard strode in wearing an EVA suit.

"Which RAM is ready for me?"

The pair glanced at one another and the trooper doing the diagnostic said, "Sir? No one said anything to us about you taking a RAM out."

The other man nodded.

Archard went to the frame that held the RAM he had used earlier in the day. "Is this one good to go?"

"It can be in five minutes," the first trooper said.

"Get hopping." Archard climbed the ladder that allowed access to the battlesuit's chest and carefully eased down in. Fortunately, the military's EVA suits were practically a second skin, and there was plenty of room. Closing the chest plate, he flexed the RAM's large fingers, then lowered the helmet and keyed his mic. "Systems check."

"Accessing the processor," the RAM's computer replied.

"Power level?"

"Ninety-eight percent."

"Weapons?"

"All systems armed, all systems functional."

"Fuel cells?"

"Eighty-seven percent."

Lower than Archard liked but still enough to keep the battlesuit aloft for hours.

The two troopers were busy disengaging the support frame and rolling it away.

"Almost ready, sir," the first trooper said.

"I'll get the door," the second offered.

The first trooper wore a puzzled expression. "May I ask a question, sir?"

"You may," Archard said.

"Why are you wearing an EVA suit inside the RAM? I mean, the RAM has its own life support. I've never seen anyone do it before."

"I have my reasons, private," Archard said. He didn't elaborate. "Let's get that door open."

Behind him, high on a wall, a speaker crackled to life. "Captain Rahn," Colonel Vasin's voice rumbled, "Report to Control."

Archard engaged the RAM and thumped to the bottom of the ramp that led up to street level.

The second trooper kept glancing from Archard to the speaker and back again.

"The door," Archard commanded.

Nodding, the trooper complied. The corrugated metal clanked and creaked until it was all the way up.

"Captain Rahn," the speaker blared anew. "Report to Control immediately."

"Isn't that you, sir?" the second trooper said.

"I heard, private," Archard said. "I'll contact them once I'm outside."

Just not immediately, Archard told himself. Thunking up the ramp, he wasted no time in going airborne. It was two blocks to an airlock large enough for the RAM. Worried the colonel might seal the locks to prevent him from leaving, he engaged his thrusters.

Civilians raised their heads and pointed and beamed.

Archard wasted no time. Landing, he opened the inner airlock door, ducked slightly, and stepped in. He was forced to wait while the inner door closed and the lock was pressurized. Only then would the outer door open. Impatient, he tapped his fingers against the battlesuit, the ping of the metallic alloy loud in the lock's confines.

Archard exhaled in relief when he was finally able to emerge. Again, he took to the air and flew around the dome, making for the hangar.

That was when his helmet's headset flared to life.

"Captain Rahn, this is Colonel Vasin. You will acknowledge this instant. That's an order."

"Colonel," Archard said.

"What in heaven's name do you think you're doing, Captain?"

"Sir?" Archard said.

"Don't play dumb. I'm in the Control Center. I see a RAM outside the dome, and your locator chip tells me that you're in it."

"Yes, sir," Archard said. There was no sense in denying it.

"What the hell?" Colonel Vasin said. "You're supposed to be here with me."

"I've decided to escort the Thunderbolt," Archard said.

"You will do no such thing," Colonel Vasin said. "General Augusto ordered you to refrain from placing yourself in harm's way. I was there when he told you, remember?"

"Yes, sir."

"Turn around and report to HQ."

Archard steeled himself. "No, sir, I will not."

"The general will have your bars for this."

"Possibly, sir." Archard cleared the dome and saw the hangar in the distance. Rising above it, gleaming silver in the Martian sunlight, was the Thunderbolt.

"Damn it, Captain. What are you playing at?"

"I'm hardly playing, sir," Archard said. "I was put in charge of this op. To that end, I've determined that the wisest recourse is for me to oversee things while in the field. Not from here."

"General Augusto would call this putting yourself at risk."

"A low risk, with me in the RAM."

"You're quibbling, Captain," the colonel said. "I doubt the general will be very much amused."

"I've made up my mind," Archard said. "What I need to know is if you will help me or hinder me, sir?"

When no reply was forthcoming, Archard said again, "Sir?"

"As much as I would like to toss you in the brig, you've given me no choice," Colonel Vasin said. "I'd have to send the other RAM units out after you, and if you still refused to return, what then? Have them blow you out of the air? No. You've hamstrung me nicely. You have my full support until you return."

"Thank you, sir," Archard said.

"I wasn't done. I intend to bring you up on charges. And there is no telling what the general will do." Colonel Vasin paused. "Do you still think this gambit of yours is worth it?"

Archard chuckled. "It will give me something to look forward to when I get back."

9

KLL-12 brought their ship down in the shadow of the towering cone of Albor Tholus. Their craft raised a dust cloud as it settled. As the thrum of the propulsion system faded, he switched on the external speakers and heard the swish of the Martian wind on the hull.

"Here we are on another planet," KLL-13 declared from her seat beside him.

"Obviously," KLL-12 said.

"Aren't you excited?"

"No."

KLL-13 swiveled toward him and chuckled. "They must have grown you under a rock instead of in a test-tube like the rest of us."

"I don't understand the allusion," KLL-12 admitted.

"Your emotions," KLL-13 teased. "Where are they?"

"Emotion is a hindrance," KLL-12 told her. "It prevents us from performing at optimal levels."

"Oh brother," KLL-13 said.

"I keep mine under complete control."

"Really? I'd never have guessed." She laughed, then stretched. "It's interesting, isn't it? The variables in our makeups? Our bodies are the same, our intellects equal, yet emotionally, some of us are more expressive than others."

"Blame the humans."

KLL-13 leaned back, appraising him. "Is it me or do you find a lot of fault with them?"

"They rushed us into production," KLL-12 reminded her. "Uniformity was sacrificed for the sake of expediency."

"You make us sound like machines," KLL-13 said. "We're not. We're organic. Biologically engineered to be the ultimate warriors."

"Created in test tubes and grown in vats," KLL-12 said. "A production process not much different from how they grow their vegetables."

"I'm proud to be a BioMarine," KLL-13 said. "Aren't you?"

"Pride is an emotion."

"You must feel something," she said. "Reach deep inside yourself and let your emotions out. You'll find life a lot more enjoyable."

"Now is hardly the time to indulge in such silliness," KLL-12 said.

Just then the console beeped and chirped, relaying a coded message.

"The signal," KLL-13 said. "It's time."

"Let's hope the humans merit your faith in them," KLL-12 said, "or in a very short while, we will both be dead."

10

Mixed emotions tore at Archard. On the one hand, it felt great to be out in the field again, to actually be doing something instead of anxiously waiting in Bradbury for the attack he was certain was inevitable.

His RAM's thrusters roaring, he cleaved the air like some Titan of old. Off to one side, the Thunderbolt kept pace. The craft could easily leave him in the Martian dust, as it were, but as he had made plain to Lieutenant Burroughs, they were joined at the hip, again as it were, until the op was over.

Bradbury was ten kilometers behind them. They were soaring over exceptionally broken terrain, the result of a geologic upheaval in the distant past.

Archard had his sensors pegged to the max. He was on the lookout for a cave or any other entrance into the underground domain of the Martians. The problem was, the Martians were ingeniously adept at camouflage. Seemingly solid boulders or rock columns might hide a means of ingress.

"Anything on your end, Lieutenant?" Archard said into his helmet mic. The Thunderbolt's sensor array was superior to the RAM's.

"Not yet, sir," Burroughs replied.

Archard switched to the frequency to U.N.I.C. HQ. "Colonel Vasin, do you copy?"

"Affirmative, Captain."

"I'd like you to do me a favor, if you would."

Vasin's snort was so loud, it was as if he were right there. "You have your nerve. You're in direct violation of the general's orders and you refused to obey mine to return to the colony. Yet now you want a favor?" Vasin snorted a second time.

"I would be very grateful if you would get word to Dr. Katla Dkany. I was supposed to meet her half an hour ago and she might be worried."

"Oh, she's worried, all right," Colonel Vasin said.

"Sir?"

"She called HQ and wanted to be put in touch with you," Colonel Vasin said. "I explained that the next time she gets to see you will be in the brig."

"Was that really necessary, sir?" Archard said, miffed.

"Captain, you seem to have forgotten that the United Nations Interplanetary Command is a military organization. We do not tolerate breaches of discipline as severe as yours. It's unbelievable to me that you---"

Archard was in no mood for a lecture. Fortunately, his commlink crackled with an excited cry from Lieutenant Burroughs.

"Movement, Captain. Half a kilometer ahead, at ten o'clock. Do you see that spire?"

"Sir, have to go," Archard cut Vasin off. Increasing the magnification on his helmet's holo display, he zeroed in on the spire. At first glance, it appeared no different from others that dotted the Martian landscape. But when he boosted the magnification even more, he noticed an oddly smooth section at the bottom.

"We picked up something moving toward it," Burroughs had gone on. "Ripples of motion, like at Wellsville."

"The ripples disappeared near the spire?"

"They did," she confirmed.

"Bingo," Archard said and smiled. "Are your people suited up and ready to go?"

"Raring for action, sir."

"Good," Archard said. "We're about to get more than they can imagine."

11

The moment of truth, as the humans would say, had come.

"I will go first," KLL-12 said. There was only room in the airlock for one of them at a time. He pressed the button to open the inner door.

"Noble of you," KLL-13 said.

"I am senior. It is my right."

"I thought you were doing it to spare me from possible harm in case something goes wrong," KLL-13 said in that ingratiatingly sweet manner she had.

"Romance is for humans," KLL-12 said.

"You seem to forget that you are part human, yourself, buster," KLL-13 said.

"Don't remind me." KLL-12 would have said more but the door slid wide and he stepped in and hit the button to close it.

He heard her laugh.

KLL-12 caught sight of himself in the mirror-finish of the airlock. At over three meters in height and weighing in excess of two hundred and twenty kilograms, with his scales and claws and ears that came to a point and his copper-colored hide, he bore no resemblance to his creators. Nor would he want to. Humans were puny things, as weak and frail as their own infants. Yet more reason to feel about them as he did.

A loud hiss sounded. Martian air was being pumped in to equalize the pressure so the outer door could be safely opened.

KLL-12 felt tremendous unease. Yes, the humans had bioengineered him and those like him to be their ultimate weapons. Yes, the BioMarines possessed abilities far beyond those of their creators. But those same creators were fallible.

What if, in human parlance, they had screwed up?

Suddenly, his chest felt as if it were in the grip of an iron fist. KLL-12 let out a gasp. The change in atmospheres was drastic, the pressure on Mars only about one percent of that of Earth at sea level. He could feel the slits on the side of his neck---his gills---expanding and contracting in an effort to get more air into his lungs. He took a breath, or tried to. The constriction in his chest worsened. His consciousness dimmed, and he thought he would pass out.

Struggling mightily, KLL-12 stabbed the button to open the outer door. If he were going to die, then he would do it outside, not trapped in the airlock.

The door opened with aggravating slowness.

KLL-12 stuck his head out and gulped noisily, his nose and gills both flaring. The pressure in his chest eased a little. Grasping the edge of the door, he blinked in the pale Martian sunlight. The intensity was only about half of that of Earth, but his eyes needed to adjust from the dim illumination of the spaceship.

The door opened wider. KLL-12 lurched from the airlock and straightened. He could feel a breeze on his scales; he could smell the Martian dust. His breathing stabilized.

A giddiness came over him, a sense of delight such as he had never experienced. Spreading his arms, KLL-12 savored the sensation of pure and simple life.

The humans had succeeded, after all.

His body was working as it should.

The tiny chip subcutaneously embedded behind his left ear chirped and he pressed the spot to activate the link.

"....are you there, handsome? Can you hear me?" KLL-13 anxiously asked. "Did you survive?"

"I am well," KLL-12 said.

Her laughter this time pleased him.

"Look out, Mars! The BioMarines have landed! I'll be right out to join you and we can start kicking Martian ass."

"Must you?" KLL-12 said.

"Must I what?" she said.

12

As a precaution, Archard stayed airborne while the Thunderbolt landed. If they were right about the spire, countless Martians might dwell somewhere under it. Not until Lieutenant Burroughs and her strike team had emerged in their EVA suits and formed up with their Individual Combat Weapons at the ready did he reduce his thrusters and descend.

The RAM came down with a loud thump. Facing the junior officer and her four troopers, Archard said, "Everyone locked and loaded?"

"Need you ask, sir?" Private Everett responded. Smirking, he patted his ICW. "I was born locked and loaded."

Private Keller laughed.

"We're as ready as we'll ever be," Lieutenant Burroughs said. An extra ICW was slung over her left shoulder.

"Listen up," Archard addressed them. "The lieutenant, Sergeant Kline, and Private Everett have fought the Martians before so they know what to expect. Private Stratton, Private Keller, you haven't. Keep close to the others and watch your backs."

"That goes without saying, sir," Private Stratton said.

Archard supposed it did. Turning, he moved to the base of the spire and examined the presumed entryway close up. It appeared to be solid rock, with no openings.

Bunching the battlesuit's massive right fist, he struck the spire with all the RAM's might. A spider's web of cracks blossomed. Drawing back his fist, he struck it again, and yet a third time, the boom of his blows resounding like thunder.

Whatever substance the 'door' was composed of---Archard was of the opinion it was some sort of artificial stone---buckled. Inserting his metal fingers into the largest cracks, he pried and pulled until he exposed the dark maw of a tunnel.

"Look out, Martians, here we come!" Private Stratton said.

Bending, Archard switched on his helmet spotlight. As he expected, the tunnel wasn't high enough or wide enough for the RAM. Stepping back, he straightened.

"We'll have to leave the battlesuit here."

"So that's why you're wearing an EVA suit inside it, sir?" Private Everett said. "I was stumped as to what you were up to. Mighty clever."

"Enough chatter," Lieutenant Burroughs said. "From here on out, maintain radio silence except as necessary. That goes for all of you."

Archard put the RAM in sleep mode and opened the chest plate. Without a ladder, he had to hang from the bottom of the opening and drop to the ground.

"Here you go, sir." Lieutenant Burroughs held out the extra ICW. "Just like you planned."

Experience had taught Archard most Martian tunnels weren't large enough for the battlesuit. He could have flown in the Thunderbolt with the rest of the ops team, but the RAM gave them added firepower should they be forced to retreat with the creatures breathing down their necks.

"Let's do this," Archard said. He brought up the holo display on his EVA helmet, in reality a form-fitting skullcap that expanded to enclose his entire head. He also turned on his spotlight. "Remember," he said. "The creatures don't show up on infrared. They don't have heat signatures like we do."

"That's why you keep your motion sensors at max," Lieutenant Burroughs instructed the others. "It's the only way we can detect them."

Hefting his ICW, Archard warily entered. Burroughs immediately glued herself to his side. The rest followed, two by two.

Deep scratch marks on the sides and overhead reminded Archard that the creatures, like spiders, were capable of scaling sheer walls and hanging from a ceiling. "Who has the locator beacons?"

"I do, sir," Sergeant Kline said.

"Plant one every two hundred meters," Archard directed. No larger than small coins, the L.B.s would keep them from becoming lost in the underground maze they were sure to encounter.

A deathly stillness prevailed. No sounds reached them, either from above or rose from below.

"Feels like a tomb," Private Stratton muttered.

"What did I tell you about talking?" Lieutenant Burroughs said. Suddenly stiffening, she exclaimed, "Picking up motion."

Archard checked his own holo, but nothing. "How far in?"

"Fifty meters or so. It was there and it was gone."

"Single file," Archard commanded, "with Private Everett bringing up the rear."

They assumed the new formation.

Sweeping his spotlight from side to side, Archard advanced toward a darker area on the left wall. It resolved into a junction. Raising a fist to signal the others to halt, he crept forward and poked his head around the bend.

What he saw caused him to doubt his own senses.

13

Had there been humans to witness the ascent, those humans would have been in awe.

KLL-12 and KLL-13 were literal blurs as they scaled the volcano's gigantic cone. Able to find purchase where humans couldn't, their biogenetically engineered forms appeared to flow up Albor Tholus. All without the aid of a single rope or carabiner.

KLL-12 reveled in his strength and speed. Seldom was he able to cut loose like this. Their creators had put them through interminable training sessions but he had never really had much of a chance to unleash his full potential.

KLL-13's laughter pealed in his subcutaneous commlink.

"What now?" he said.

"Don't tell me you're not as exhilarated as I am," she replied.

"We're scaling a volcano," KLL-12 made light of their feat.

"I swear," she said.

Springing to a higher handhold, KLL-12 paused to survey the sweeping vista below. They were about midway up the cone, nearly two and a quarter kilometers above the Martian surface. The view was spectacular.

KLL-13 stopped when he did. "Magnificent, isn't it?"

"Rocks and dirt," KLL-12 said. "What's so special about that?"

"You have no poetry in your soul."

"I have no soul, period," KLL-12 set her straight. Nor, he was convinced, did the humans, despite the convictions of many among them.

"You don't know that," KLL-13 said.

"Prove to me we do."

"Here and now?"

"The simple truth is you can't," KLL-12 said. "Which is just as well. Unlike our human creators, I'm not desirous of living forever."

"Maybe your birthing vat had a crack in it," KLL-13 said. "That would explain a lot."

KLL-12 was about to ask what she meant when he detected a faint buzzing from far above. Tilting his head back, he spied half a dozen dark specks rising out of the volcano. In a tight group, they swept over the rim and went into a dive.

"Martians with wings!" KLL-13 exclaimed.

"Captain Archard Rahn mentioned encountering them in his report," KLL-12 remembered from their briefing prior to their departure from Earth. "Flyers, he called them."

"They're heading straight for us!" KLL-13 said. "How do they know we're here?"

"They probably heard you flapping your gums."

"Did you just make a joke?"

KLL-12 looked down. His companion was grinning from ear to her, her razor teeth a white against the copper of her scales. "At a time like this? The utmost seriousness is called for."

"Life is too short to be serious about anything," KLL-13 said.

His eyes on the Martians, KLL-12 resumed climbing. Based on his estimate of their speed and the distance they must travel, he calculated it wouldn't take the creatures more than two minutes to reach them.

"Our first fight!" KLL-13 said cheerfully.

KLL-12 would rather they weren't clinging to the rock cone. He glanced about for a better vantage point and spotted a meter-wide projection about twenty meters long. Pointing, he called out, "There! A ledge!"

KLL-13 nodded.

Together, they poured on the speed. Together, they scrambled up and over the ledge and stood with their backs to the cone.

"There isn't much room to maneuver," KLL-12 said.

"Enough to kill," KLL-13 said, and flexed her claw-capped fingers.

The creatures were a lot closer. They were exactly as Captain Rahn had described them; black carapaces, eight pair of stubby wings and a pair of forelimbs that ended in spikes capable of punching a hole in a RAM. The captain had made it plain that their thick shells and incredible speed made them hard to slay.

KLL-13 nodded at the abyss. "If they knock us off, we better hope our membranes work."

"Is that doubt I hear?" KLL-12 said. "I thought our creators are infallible."

"Bite me."

"I'll leave that to the Martians," KLL-12 said.

Further talk was nipped in the bud by the arrival of their attackers. Buzzing noisily, the creatures streaked out and in, coming at them head-on.

KLL-12 had no time to think, no time for anything except to react on the most instinctual level. The foremost extended its spikes and closed on him, and he twisted to evade them and swatted the creature's forelimbs aside. The Martian was on him again in a heartbeat. Instantly, he backhanded it with his fist, striking a ridge that ran along the front of its carapace. The force of his blow knocked the flyer back into two others.

Quickly recovering, they regained altitude.

KLL-12 was aware that KLL-13 was battling for her life but he couldn't divert his attention to help her. Already the three Martians were angling toward him, their spikes as rigid as spears. He might avoid one or two but not all three.

KLL-12 did the last thing any being would expect. Bounding high into the air, he landed on top of the middle Martian. Before it could think to flip him off, he flashed his claws in a windmill of ferocity. The creature's carapace withstood his assault for all of five seconds. Then a green ochre spurted and went on spurting, splashing his arms and chest.

The creature went limp and dropped but KLL-12 was already in motion. A prodigious leap, timed perfectly, carried him to a second Martian. Grabbing at its uppermost wings, he gained a hold, only to have the creature buck like a wild horse trying to throw its rider. Again KLL-12 used his claws like scythes, ripping and rending in abandon. Its organs, or what passed for them---tubular bits and ovoid pieces and cord-like filaments---spilled out.

The creature started to lose altitude.

Once more, KLL-12 leaped, this time toward the cone. He snagged a crack wide enough for his fingers and hung suspended by one arm. Above him, KLL-13 was still on the ledge, battling fiercely.

For a few moments, KLL-12 let himself be distracted by her fight, and it cost him. Without any forewarning, a Martian flyer slammed into his back.

14

No one on Mars knew more about the Martians than Archard. He had encountered every kind---or so he thought. There were the yellow ones, the rarest, that he took to be their leaders. There were the reddish crab-like workers, or soldiers. There were the huge blue warriors. There were the gigantic drillers. And the flyers.

The creature he now beheld was so different, he stood riveted in astonishment.

The thing resembled a slug on steroids. Two meters wide and five meters long, it had an orange carapace much like those of the other Martians. Except that this creature was covered in slime---or was it mucus?---from one end to the other. It didn't have legs or forelimbs or wings, only four long antennae, if that is what they were. At the end of the four long rods were large black eyes that waved back and forth and up and down.

It was unlike any of the other Martians.

The thing had turned broadside and was making loud squishing noises as it sucked at the dusty tunnel floor with a mouth as long and flexible as an elephant seal's snout.

Bewildered, Archard raised his ICW but didn't fire. The thing posed no immediate threat, and the shots might bring others. He hoped it would go its merry way along the side branch. But as if it somehow sensed his presence, the creature raised its four long stalks and swung its four black eyes in his direction.

"Hell," Archard said under his breath. He braced for an attack but unexpectedly a new element broke onto the scene---literally.

Above and beyond the slug, a small hole suddenly appeared. It swiftly widened. Bits and pieces of rock rained down, pattering like hail. Reddish-pink limbs protruded, appendages with crab-like grippers that were tearing at the solid stone as if it were tissue paper. In moments, the hole was wide enough that the creature making it scrabbled out of the opening and down the tunnel wall, moving like an oversized spider. Behind it came another and then more, seven, eight, nine, and still they came.

Martians. To be precise, the 'worker' or 'soldier' Martians. They were the most common, and the smallest, barely a meter round. They were also savage beyond belief.

Archard was about to turn and shout into his commlink for Lieutenant Burroughs and the strike team to prepare for an assault when yet another unexpected occurrence kept him glued where he was.

The crabs attacked the slug.

The slime-covered creature had sensed or heard the rain of rocks and shifted its massive bulk toward the newcomers. Its giant body rippling, it started to back away but the soldiers were on it in a rush, swarming up and over its slimy mass like army ants swarming a lizard.

The slug erupted into violent motion, bucking and heaving, seeking to throw the Martians off. Several went flying but most clung fast with their grippers. Changing tactics, the slug slammed its body against the tunnel walls, smashing Martians to pulp. It succeeded in slaying half a dozen. But that was nowhere near enough.

Over forty Martians now covered the slug, all of them ripping and tearing at its carapace to get at the flesh underneath. Sprays of purple blood turned into gaping wounds.

The slug fought for dear life but was overwhelmed by sheer numbers. The Martians rendered its body into pieces and sections, much as humans might butcher a cow. At least, that was the analogy that popped into Archard's head as he watched the slug suddenly extend its snout, give a last convulsive shake, and collapse.

"Captain?"

The crackle of his helmet nearly made Archard jump. He had been so intent on the slaughter, he'd neglected to alert the others. "Lieutenant Burroughs..." he began and stopped.

The Martians were spreading out.

Archard realized he should have gotten out of there while he had the chance. His mistake might prove costly. If he and the others were discovered, the Martians would be on them in a flash.

"Captain?" Lieutenant Burroughs said again. "Is everything all right?"

Archard saw a Martian scuttling toward the junction. "Not hardly," he said.

15

The Earth fleet decelerated out of EmDrive and assumed a stationary orbit over Bradbury, appearing like great silver stars out of the dark ether of space. One instant they weren't there, the next they were.

General Constantine Augusto surveyed the three immense golden domes on the *Avenger I*'s view screen and grunted in satisfaction. "They're still there."

Admiral Thorndyke, standing beside the command chair that General Augusto had appropriated, didn't hide his surprise. "You thought they wouldn't be?"

"Why else did I rush things like a madman back on Earth?" General Augusto said. He didn't wait for an answer. "We'd lost two colonies, and I'll be damned if we'll lose a third. I expedited the provisioning and armaments procurement for our fleet so that we could reach Mars in record time. Which we have," he concluded proudly.

The communications officer raised her head from her console. "General Augusto, Governor Bradbury is on line four. He would very much like to speak to you."

"Would he now?" General Augusto said. "On speakers."

The governor's voice was tinny and laced with static. "General Augusto? Are you there?"

"If I'm not, you're talking to yourself," General Augusto said. "Eh?"

"What do you want, Governor?"

"I've just been notified that you're here already. The fleet, I mean. We weren't expecting you for another week and a half."

"We teleported," General Augusto said.

"General?"

"A joke, governor."

"I'm afraid I don't get the allusion."

"That's all right, Governor," General Augusto said. "What you need to do is snap out of your lethargy. Yes, I am here, and I'm assuming complete command of all Martian personal, military and civilian, for the duration. Until this crisis is resolved, you will follow my orders explicitly. Is that understood?"

"The secretary-general, in fact, notified me that you---" Blanchard started to say a trifle indignantly.

"Good," General Augusto cut him short. "Our drop ships will be landing within the hour. I want you and Colonel Vasin and Captain Archard on hand at Dome One when I arrive."

"About that," Governor Blanchard said.

"Yes?"

"Perhaps you should speak to Colonel Vasin."

"I'm speaking to you," General Augusto said. "And I don't like vacillation."

Governor Blanchard coughed a couple of times. "Captain Archard won't be able to greet you."

"Why the hell not?"

"He's not here."

"How's that again? I gave specific orders."

"The good captain accompanied the strike team on their mission. Colonel Vasin is quite upset about it."

General Augusto rose out of his chair, his fists clenched. "The devil you say? The colonel didn't see fit to let me know?"

"He probably figured it was best to wait until you arrived."

"He was wrong. I'll deal with him when I land. As for Captain Rahn, I made it plain that he's the single-most valuable resource we have on the Martians."

"Apparently he felt his proper place was with his troopers."

"You have a GPS fix on their chip implants?"

"Colonel Vasin does, I believe, yes."

"Have him relay the coordinates, ASAP," General Augusto ordered. He motioned at the communications officer and she broke the connection. "Get me the *BIO-M*," he said, referring to another ship in the fleet.

Not ten seconds elapsed and a deep voice acknowledged, "This is KLL-1, General. Our drop ships are about ready, per your orders."

"Excellent," General Augusto said. "In a minute or two, I'll send you some coordinates. You're to take your unit and assist a special ops teams in extracting a Martian prisoner."

"All of us, sir?" KLL-1 said. "They require that many?"

General Augusto chuckled. "Don't get cocky."

"Cockiness is a human trait," KLL-1 said. "I prefer to think of us as supremely confident."

"You should be," General Augusto said. "You're Marines."

"BioMarines, sir," KLL-1 amended.

"Booyah," General Augusto said. "Now get cracking."

"Sir?" KLL-1 said.

"What is it?"

"Has there been any word from KLL-12 and KLL-13? The rest of us have been wondering."

"They were under orders to maintain radio silence," General Augusto said. "For all I know, the Martians might be able to monitor our commlinks."

"I hope all is well with them."

"You and me both," General Augusto said.

16

The Martian flyer thrust a forelimb spike into KLL-12 between his shoulder blades.

If his heart had been where a human's would be, KLL-12 would have died. As it was, even with the pain inhibitors genetically encoded into his body's nervous system, the discomfort was excruciating.

Reacting instinctively, KLL-12 whipped around, seized the flyer, and smashed it against the cone. Given his immense strength, that should have been enough to slay it. But no. The thing's other forelimb lanced at his neck. He saved himself by grabbing hold of the spike.

Locked together, they struggled, bio-engineered construct against an alien lifeform. The outcome hung in doubt until suddenly a scale-covered copper figure hurtled down from above and landed on top of the Flyer. Gore-smeared claws tore at its wings, ripping them off as if they were a butterfly's. The Martian was yanked loose of KLL-12 and cast down.

Tumbling as it plummeted, the creature never made a sound. When it struck, far, far below, it was no more than a black speck against the backdrop of ground.

Clinging by one hand from a crack, KLL-13 grinned and said, "Miss me?"

"I didn't require your aid," KLL-12 said.

"You're welcome," KLL-13 said. Tilting, she examined his back. "That looks nasty but it's already healing."

"It is supposed to," KLL-12 reminded her. Their accelerated healing factor was yet another of the biological upgrades incorporated into their bodies by their creators.

"Do you feel anything? Pain, I mean?"

"Very little."

"The humans did a good job with us. You have to admit."

"We are as we were designed," KLL-12 said. Levering his toe into a gap, he resumed their climb. "We should try to reach the top before the Martians send more flyers."

"Fine by me," KLL-13 said, "although it was fun kicking their asses."

KLL-12 flowed upward, moving as fast as ever. He could feel his flesh reknitting itself, feel new scales sprouting to replace those lost.

KLL-13 effortlessly kept pace.

Not until they were within fifty meters of the top did KLL-12 stop. "Do you need to rest before the next phase?"

"Be serious," she said. "We're BioMarines."

"It has been a long climb."

"And we're not even winded. Have to hand it to those humans, don't we?"

"Why do you keep bringing that up?"

"Because you seem to have forgotten we wouldn't exist if not for them."

"I would prefer not to be reminded," KLL-12 said.

To forestall her from continuing to carp about their creators, he put on a burst of speed and reached the rim. It turned out to be ten meters wide. Moving to the inner edge, he peered into the darkling depths of the volcano.

"Spooky," KLL-13 said.

"We'll use our membranes," KLL-12 said.

"This will be fun."

Ignoring her, KLL-12 raised his arms straight up, closed his eyes, and concentrated. He felt a slight tug, and when he opened his eyes, he found that both membranes had snapped free from under his arms and along his sides.

KLL-13 had imitated him and giggled. "Do you know what these remind me of?"

"Glider wings," KLL-12 said, since that's what they were.

"Squirrels," KLL-13 said.

"You're comparing us to tree-climbing rodents?"

"Flying squirrels have membranes similar to ours. I sometimes wonder if that's where our creators got the idea."

"The tensile strength of ours is that of organic steel," KLL-12 said. "We're superior to those rodents in every way."

"They're better at collecting nuts," KLL-13 said and winked. "Or maybe not."

"By nut do you mean me?"

"If the shell fits," she said.

KLL-12 launched himself over the edge. Her laughter followed him as he banked at the proper angle for a controlled descent. The push of air against his membranes was considerable. His arms fluttered a couple of times but he maintained control and swooped in a spiral that would take him steadily lower.

They had a long way to go. According to intel gleaned by Captain Archard Rahn and passed on to U.N.I.C. headquarters on Earth, the Martian warren was two kilometers underground.

The caldera itself was wide---thirty kilometers across. Updrafts were frequent. So were crosscurrents that threatened to upend them.

"Isn't this glorious?" KLL-13 said over their commlink.

"Radio silence, if you please," KLL-12 said.

"They know we're here. We just killed a bunch of them."

"Perhaps those we slew weren't able to alert the others."

"Who would have thought that deep down you're an optimist," KLL-13 said with her usual laugh.

Their enhanced sight enabled them to see in the dark as if it were the brightest day. Consequently, KLL-12 spotted the dark cloud roiling up out of the volcano's depths when it was still a great distance below. "More flyers."

"Must be a hundred or better," KLL-13 said. "How will we handle that many?"

"Follow my lead," KLL-12, and tilted his body to increase his speed.

17

Miles Hermann was in a bad mood. His boss, Governor Blanchard, was being a horse's ass. All because the United Nations Security Council had appointed General Constantine Augusto as Supreme Martian Commander for the duration of hostilities. Civil liberties had been curtailed. Emergency sanctions---a polite term for martial law---had been imposed, and Governor Blanchard had been relegated to the status of a glorified errand boy.

Predictably, the governor was taking his spite out on everyone around and under him, including Miles.

Half an hour ago, a call had come in from the Water Conversion Plant, a problem of some kind that the plant manager insisted required Governor Blanchard's personal attention.

"One of the converters is probably on the fritz," Blanchard had said to Miles after taking the call. He'd shaken his head, and swore. "I doubt they really need me there. You tend to it, Miles."

"Me?" Miles had bleated. He'd been to the plant a few times but knew next to nothing about how the Martian water was extracted and converted for human use. He was in admin, for crying out loud, not a scientist or a technician.

"Yes, you," Governor Blanchard snipped and wriggled his fingers to speed Miles on his way.

Now here Miles was, approaching the Water Conversion Plant on foot since he didn't have the nerve to ask Blanchard if it would be all right to use the limo.

Miles became aware that passers-by were stopping and craning their necks and pointing. Coming to a halt, he bent his own head back.

Drop ships were descending from the fleet. Like so many hornets leaving their nest, they separated from their mother craft and literally dropped---hence their name---toward the colony's golden domes. Troopers and armaments and more, coming to their rescue.

Miles supposed he should be as happy and excited as everyone else but he was too upset at being treated like a gofer by the governor. Five years he had worked for that man. Five years, getting his coffee and seeing that he always had a water bottle in his second drawer on the left. Five years! And it counted for nothing.

Grumbling at how unfair life could be, Miles reached the plant entrance and punched the code to open the door. The facility was crucial to the colony's survival, which was why only the staff and certain higher-ups, like Miles, were allowed free run of the place.

The door chimed and clanged, and the halves swung inward. Entering, Miles crossed to the partition to the main office. He would have to sign in, as required by the regs.

With a start, Miles realized no one was on the other side. Which was odd. There was always supposed to be someone there. "Anyone home?" He rapped on the glass. "Hello?"

When no one answered, Miles pounded harder, and shouted, "This is Miles Hermann. I'm here on the governor's behalf. Where is everyone?"

There was no reply.

No one came out to greet him.

Puzzled, Miles stepped to the partition door and opened it. "Hello?" he said again. "Someone reported some kind of problem?"

Miles stopped short in consternation. The entire office staff was gone. Wondering if it might be their break time, Miles hastened along a short hall to the break room. No one was there. Strangely, several trays of food and drink were on the table, as if people had been eating and left their meals in a hurry.

"What in the world?" Miles marveled out loud. He went through the break room and out the other end and down another corridor to the double doors to the plant proper. As he pushed on one, he hollered the manager's name. "Mr. Timmons! You called for assistance. Where are you?"

Again, Miles drew up short. Before him stretched the warehouse-sized heart of the operation, consisting of huge tanks and pipes and banks of equipment. Workers should be engaged in a variety of tasks, but other than the drum of the machinery, the place was dead.

"Mr. Timmons?" Miles yelled.

His footsteps seemed unnaturally loud as he headed down an aisle between two of the giant tanks. They were transparent, and the rust-colored Martian water that was being chemically treated to render it suitable for the human body looked like so much sludge.

"Mr. Timmons? Where in the world are you?"

A metal ladder leading to a crosswalk above a tank gave Miles an idea. From up there, he would be able to see most of the plant.

Laboriously climbing, Miles came to the crosswalk and moved along it, searching. He yelled for the manager, for anyone at all, only to be mocked by silence.

"This is damn weird."

Leaning on a rail, Miles absently stared into the chemical stew. He was thinking he should report this to the governor. Having made up his mind, he straightened and went to retrace his steps but stopped on spying a smear of some kind on the plant floor about thirty meters off.

The smear was red.

"Surely not," Miles said.

A bubble rose to the surface of the tank and burst with a loud pop.

Miles paid it no mind. He was worried and wanted out of there. Pivoting, he hurried toward the ladder.

More bubbles were rising and popping.

Glancing over, it took Miles a few steps for him to realize that the bubbles were rising in a straight line---and the line was coming toward him.

Miles broke into a run. He was badly out of shape. He only ever exercised to pass his yearly exams, but he forced his legs to work and was only a couple of meters from the ladder when something---a whole lot of somethings---scrambled up out of the tank and over the top.

The red, crab-like Martians.

Miles shrieked in terror. He couldn't understand how the creatures had gotten into the Water Treatment Plant. Then he remembered that the water was pumped up from under the ground-

--which was where the Martians lived. He guessed that they had come up through the pipes and ducts.

Miles continued to shriek as the Martians swiftly overtook him. He shrieked louder as he was seized, louder still as his arms and legs were torn from his body. Then one of the creatures seized him by his head and there was a terrible tearing sensation followed by wet warmth all over his neck. His shriek faded to a gurgle as the world around him faded to black.

18

The BioMarines were genetically engineered to be the ultimate lethal weapons. That they were also biologically enhanced so they could survive in environments no human could endure was secondary. Whether it was the scorching inferno of a desert or the deepest depths of the ocean, or another planet, their bodies adapted superbly so that they could perform their primary function; to kill and kill again.

Billions were spent on their development. The cream of the human scientific crop was induced to participate. The "prototype," as they dubbed the first of the hybrids to emerge from the nutrient vats, exceeded every expectation.

"Do you realize what we've done?" an excited scientist said to the generals who witnessed the historic event.

"Yes," one of the generals replied. "We've just usurped God."

Their lethality and adaptability wasn't quite enough, though. Another element was added. Psychological conditioning. As another general once remarked, "We can't go to all this trouble and expense only to have them think they have minds of their own."

So while the BioMarines were still in their vats, they were subliminally conditioned, hour after hour, week after week, month after month, to perform as they were told---whether they wanted to or not.

Not that many would refuse an order anyway. They were bred to fight. The joy of combat was in their blood. When told to kill, they did so with relish.

None of them questioned the command imperative. Until KLL-12 came along.

He learned the full degree of his conditioning shortly after he emerged from the vat. He was instructed to enter a pen of sheep and slaughter them. To him, it seemed pointless. He had never seen sheep before but they were plainly timid, harmless creatures. He made bold to ask the major who gave him the order why he must slay them, and the major replied it was so he could familiarize himself with "the blood and guts of warfare."

KLL-12 had decided he wanted no part of it and turned to go. Or tried to. Because to his extreme bewilderment, he discovered he couldn't walk away. He had to do as he was told, his own feelings be damned.

As if his body had a mind of its own and he was only a spectator, he tore the sheep to pieces.

Was it any wonder, then, that he had such a low opinion of his makers?

He remembered those sheep as he swooped toward the rising cloud of Martian flyers, and thought of how he would much rather be back on Earth swimming in the base pool or listening to music or doing anything other than what he was doing.

But here he was, plummeting at six hundred kilometers an hour, his membranes taut, the air whistling past his scaled form. He shifted his right pupil to the side to check on KLL-13 and saw her grinning in delight.

For her sake, KLL-12 put everything else from his mind. They had been paired for this mission, and he owed it to her to be the best he could be. He must watch her back as she would watch his. Together, they could prevail. Or so their human masters told them.

"Density at max," KLL-12 said.

"Already am."

KLL-12 concentrated. The change occurred almost immediately, the hardening of his muscles until they were practically as dense as rock. The shifting of his scales was particularly noticeable; he itched all over. Lowering his head to protect his face, he dived at the center of the swarm.

The Martians were spaced so close together, it was a wonder they didn't collide. The foremost had their spikes extended, like knights of old with their lances.

"Remember," KLL-13 surprised him by saying. "One hundred and eighty seconds."

As if KLL-12 would forget. Their ability to change their density had a drawback. The drain on their bodies was so severe, they could only sustain the state for three minutes. Any longer, and they risked a debilitating fatigue that would leave them vulnerable to their enemies.

A hundred meters separated them from the swarm.

Then it was fifty.

Twenty-five.

KLL-12 heard KLL-13 let out a whoop just as they impacted with the creatures. They were moving so fast, they tore through the flyers like fists through thin air, smashing everything in their path. Carapaces folded like paper. Wings crumpled like tissues.

KLL-12 made the mistake of opening his mouth and nearly gagged when part of a wing slid partway down his throat. Hacking, he spat it out.

The impacts slowed them but not enough to prevent them from passing completely through the swarm and out the other side.

The moment they were in the clear, KLL-12 banked to regain speed. He also relaxed to spare his body the ravages of his density change.

KLL-13 materialized at his side. She was spattered with gore and Martians body bits, and grinning. "That was fun."

KLL-12 grunted.

"Tell me you didn't enjoy it."

The caldera was brightening, the result of some sort of natural phosphorescence. Far below, arches and shapes appeared.

"We're almost there," KLL-12 said.

"The Martian city!" KLL-13 exclaimed. "Imagine. We'll be only the second and third people to see one."

"Are we people?" KLL-12 asked before he could catch himself.

"What else would we be?"

KLL-12 had no time to reply. A vast cavern had unfolded before them.

A cavern filled with thousands of Martians.

19

Dr. Katla Dkany was worried. She hadn't heard from Archard since early morning when he headed off for a meeting with Governor Blanchard at the Admin Center. He'd promised to ring her as soon as it was over, but he hadn't been in touch.

Katla swiped at a loose strand of her blonde hair and rubbed the back of her neck to relieve a slight cramp. She was almost done with her chemical analysis of Martian blood swabbed from the RAM Archard wore during their arduous trek from Wellsville to Bradbury. The last day of their journey, they had been set upon, and during the battle, the RAM was splashed with gore and gouts of blood.

Katla had been given the job of analyzing the residue. As a preeminent exobiologist, she was the logical choice.

Now, after weeks of testing, Katla and her assistants were about ready to wrap things up. They had done everything from atomic absorption spectroscopy to electrophoresis, from X-ray microscopy to resonance-enhanced multiphoton ionization. In short, every conceivable type of analysis.

Katla sat back on her stool, closed her eyes, and wearily rubbed them. She had been staring into the microscope for so long, her eyes hurt. Sliding off, she smoothed her smock and made for her office at the rear of the laboratory, which was on sublevel two in the Science Center.

She should be thinking about the report she would submit but she couldn't stop fretting about Archard. Their ordeal had brought them closer than she ever imagined when they first dated. Just last night, after a pleasant meal, they had stretched out on the sofa and discussed the prospect of tying the knot upon their return to Earth.

Katla grinned to herself. She came to Mars for the adventure of a lifetime, not to find a husband. She'd planned to serve out her tour, go home, and then, maybe, find someone she was willing to spend the rest of her life with.

Her grin evaporated at the sight of the mountain of clutter on her desk. She had so much work to do. It would take several days to correlate all the data and summarize the results.

Dropping into her chair, Katla brought up an MRI image on her computer. She shook her head in amazement.

Granted, Mars was a different planet. Granted, it was logical to expect that native organisms would deviate in various respects from organisms on Earth. The Martians deviated greatly. So much so, they defied long accepted scientific tenets.

Their blood alone had proven to be an almost insurmountable challenge. There wasn't a single point of similarity between theirs and human blood except both were liquid. Theirs possessed a dynamic viscosity less than a third that of water, at a temperature of 1° Celsius. By rights, their blood should be practically frozen in their veins. Yet it flowed at a rate of three meters per second, compared to less than a meter for human beings.

Then there was the other matter, the most troubling of all, as far as Katla was concerned. Taken in total, her multitude of tests hinted at the disturbing possibility that---

There was a quick knock and in rushed one of her assistants, a young woman who hailed from Greece by the name of Cosimia. Normally, she was the picture of calm, but at the moment, she was tremendously agitated.

"Dr. Dkany," Cosimia declare. "You must come quickly."

Figuring there must have been an accident in the lab, Katla rose and came around her desk. Only then did she notice several red splotches on the front of Cosimia's smock.

"What's that?" she asked, pointing.

"Blood," the younger woman said.

"You've hurt yourself?" Katla said, looking for signs of a wound.

"No. I was taking residue down to the incinerator. I found..." Cosimia stopped.

"You found what?"

"Please come see," Cosimia said, grabbing hold of Katla's arm. "I hope I am mistaken. Please let me be mistaken. Please, please, please."

Katla let herself be pulled out into the hall and over to the elevator. Extricating her arm, she smiled and said, "You need to compose yourself."

"But it might be like you told us," Cosimia said, and there was no mistaking the fear in her eyes. "At New Meridian and then at Wellsville."

"What are you...?" Katla said, and now it was her turn to stop as the other's meaning hit home.

The elevator door opened and Cosimia entered. "Please. We must hurry. If I am right, you will know, and we can alert the troopers."

Again, Katla let herself be pulled. Horrific images of the terrors she endured at the other colonies flooded through her. She was barely aware of the elevator stopping and the door pinging open.

"Dr. Dkany? Are you all right?"

Taking a deep breath, Katla nodded and followed Cosimia down the corridor. At the far end, the door to the facility's incinerator was wide open.

"Wait," Cosimia said, halting. "I closed that."

"Maybe someone else is burning something," Katla suggested.

"No. You don't understand. They wouldn't. Come." The younger woman hurried on.

A feeling of dread welled up, a feeling so potent, so strong, Katla had to will her feet to move. She was right behind Cosimia when they reached the doorway.

Cosimia moved aside.

A gigantic barrel with a keypad for access filled most of the room. Above the barrel were the large pipes that funneled the smoke into a complicated filtration system designed to remove pollutants. Other pipes were part of a sprinkler system to be used in the event the furnace should somehow overheat.

Katla was more interested in the red smear that ran from just under the keypad to a hatch on top of a water pipe.

That hatch was open.

"God, no," Katla breathed.

"Am I right?" Cosimia said.

The answer came in the literal form of a reddish-pink creature that suddenly scrabbled up out of the hatch.

20

Captain Archard Rahn had miscalculated, badly. Martians were still coming out of the hole in the tunnel on the other side of the slug, which lay in large chunks and pieces in a spreading pool of its bizarre purple blood. The side tunnel was quickly filling with the things. It wouldn't be long before the creatures spilled into the main one.

Backpedaling, Archard keyed his commlink. "Retreat!" he barked.

"Sir?" Lieutenant Burroughs said. She and the others were waiting, single-file, their ICW's pressed to their shoulders.

"If I'm not making myself clear," Archard said, and raised his voice several notches, "Run like hell!"

United Nations Interplanetary Command troopers were some of the best-trained on Earth. They were much like the U.S. Marines of olden days, who earned a reputation the hard way for being some of the toughest mother's sons and daughters on the planet.

Ingrained into them was that when an officer gave an order, a trooper snapped to. Consequently, all five ops troopers turned and sprinted as if their lives depended on it.

"If you don't mind, sir," Lieutenant Burroughs asked as they fled, "what are we running from?"

"What else, Lieutenant?" Archard said, glancing over his shoulder. "Our mission is FUBAR'ed if we don't get of sight, and I mean now."

Troopers on Mars were required to exercise daily, and to stick to a high intake regimen of multivitamins and minerals. No exceptions. If they didn't, they lost their muscle tone, and their reflexes suffered. That wasn't all. Osteoporosis, adverse effects on the circulatory system, as well as chronic constipation and the formation of kidney stones, were endemic if the regimen wasn't followed.

Their peak fitness, and Mars' lesser gravity, enabled Archard and the others to run faster and farther than they ever could back on terra firma. Which proved fortuitous, because when Archard looked back a second time, the thing he feared had come to pass.

Martians had emerged into the main tunnel and were giving chase.

"Run faster!" Archard bawled.

There was a trick to running on Mars. Instead of pumping one's legs in a burst of short steps, running was best accomplished in carefully controlled leaps and bounds. With practice, troopers could seemingly skim the ground, their feet barely touching.

Archard skimmed for all he was worth. His motion sensors told him the Martians weren't gaining, which was strange. The creatures were ungodly quick and could outrun a human with ease. It suggested they were holding back for some reason. A reason he was sure he wouldn't like.

"How far do we go, sir?" Sergeant Kline asked from the front of the line.

"All the way out if we have to," Archard replied. Switching his helmet mic to external and then from multidirectional to unidirectional, Archard clearly picked up the scrabbling of the Martians. From the sounds, a great many were in pursuit.

"Sir," Lieutenant Burroughs broke in. "Shouldn't you and I try to delay them?"

"Indeed we should," Archard agreed. "When I say to." He waited until they negotiated a series of bends and were flying down a straight stretch. At the midway point he called out, "Here!" and stopped.

They turned and stood shoulder-to-shoulder. The others kept going.

"Frags," Archard said.

"You got it," Burroughs responded.

Archard's holo display gave him the exact distance to the last bend. "Range, thirty-five meters."

"Setting detonation at thirty-five."

Their spider-like limbs flying, Martians clattered into view. The rat-tat-tat of their bony legs on the rock walls and ceiling was like the beating of so many hammers. They were so packed together, they jostled one another in their eagerness to reach their quarry.

"Now!" Archard said, and let fly. He barely heard the *thrump* of the launcher but he definitely felt the kick of the stock.

Lieutenant Burroughs fired her own grenade.

"Down!" Archard cried, and flung himself flat. The kill radius was fifteen meters but he wasn't taking any chances. Shrapnel had been known to ricochet.

Burroughs threw herself down next to him, her forearms cushioning her face.

Almost too late, Archard remembered to mute the volume on his helmet. As it was, the twin blasts were so loud, pain lanced his ears.

The explosions shredded the leading Martians and reduced many behind them to shattered husks.

Archard was on his feet before the sounds died. Burroughs was already up, and together they spun and continued their race for life. Archard knew the creatures wouldn't give up. His team would have to make a stand, and the best place for that was outside.

A bright oval marked the end of the tunnel. The others--- Sergeant Kline, and Privates Everett, Keller and Stratton, had stopped and were looking back.

"Defensive formation!" Archard commanded. "Cover us as we come out."

He took another glance back. The Martians were further behind but coming relentlessly on.

Archard was starting to breathe heavily when he burst into the pale sunlight. The others had formed into a half-circle facing the tunnel. He and Burroughs were quick to join them. "Frag grenades," he called out. He was thinking that maybe they could bring the tunnel down on top of the Martians. It would put an end to their mission but they could always try again later.

"Sir!" Private Everett suddenly hollered. "Behind us."

Archard looked. His RAM was twenty meters away, and near it, the Thunderbolt. Beyond was a low rise, and flowing over it a living tide of Martians.

21

Not again! Dr. Katla Dkany's mind screamed as another of the crab-like Martians scrambled out of the hatch. She had lived through the fall of two colonies, had seen ghastly atrocities that teetered her mind on the brink of sanity, including people having their arms and legs and heads ripped off, and now, despite the precautions taken by the third colony's leaders, it was about to happen all over again.

Whirling, Katla pushed Cosimia. "Run!" she screamed.

The Greek chemist needed no urging. On wings of fear she flew from the incinerator room, Katla close behind.

Too late, Katla thought to close the incinerator door. Not that it would stop the Martians for long.

Breathless, they reached the elevator. The indicator panel revealed it was on an upper floor, and climbing.

"We can't wait," Katla said, and dashed to the stairwell. The door resisted. For a few harrowing moments, she feared it was locked or jammed. She put her shoulder to it and strained, and almost yipped for joy when it opened. "Follow me!"

Their feet pattered noisily as they climbed.

Katla kept glancing down, expecting at any second that the Martians would appear. Strangely, they didn't. She and Cosimia gained the next floor safely, and kept going.

"Dr. Dkany?" Cosimia said.

"We need to warn everyone," Katla puffed. The main office on the ground floor was their best bet. She would use the intercom and alert every lab and office in the Science Center. A mass evacuation was called for.

When they reached the landing, Katla jerked the door wide and flew toward the office, shoving people who were in her way. "Run!" she cried. "Vacate the building! The Martians are here!"

Amazingly, few heeded her. Most looked perplexed, as if they thought she couldn't be serious.

"Tell them!" Katla shouted at Cosimia. She rounded a column, avoided an artificial fern, and collided with a broad figure with a bulbous nose who was just coming out of the office. The impact knocked her back a couple of steps and she almost lost her balance.

"Dr. Dkany? What in the world?"

Katla realized she had barreled into the head of the Science Center. "Dr. Huffington!" she gasped. "The Martians!"

"What about them?" Huffington said. In his late forties, he sported greying sideburns and a Van Dyke. He was wearing a suit and had a briefcase in his left hand.

"They're here!" Rushing to him and placing her hands on his chest, she said, "You have to warn everyone!"

"They're where?" Huffington said.

"Here!" Katla pointed at the floor. "In this very building. Down in the incinerator room."

"What's that? Are you joking?"

Incredulous that he would think she was making it up, Katla gripped his shirt and shook him. "Aren't you listening? The Martians are in Bradbury! We have to tell everyone. We have to inform the U.N.I.C."

"Hold on," Huffington said. He glanced at passers-by who had stopped to listen, gripped her by the wrist, and ushered her into the office.

Katla didn't resist. "Get on the horn. Alert everyone before it's too late."

"Hold on," Huffington said again. "Start at the beginning. You say there are Martians in the incinerator room? What would they be doing there?"

Angry now, Katla wrenched her hand loose. "Don't you get it? They've found a way into the colony. Underground, just like at New Meridian and Wellsville."

"But the governor has taken steps," Huffington said with aggravating calm. "Installed motion sensors and cameras that constantly monitored. There's been no sign of anything unusual."

Katla could have slugged him. "Damn it. Are you calling me a liar?"

"No," Huffington said, although his tone suggested he still didn't entirely believe her. "Look. General Augusto has landed and his troops are entering the domes. I'll put a call through and ask him to send soldiers to investigate. How does that sound?"

"It's a start," Katla said. But her gut told her it was nowhere near enough.

22

KLL-12 felt his membranes vibrate as he banked to gain a panoramic view of a cavern so immense, its sides were lost in the distance. Immense, too, was the Martian metropolis that nearly filled it, an underground city that could be summed up by saying it was "otherworldly." To put it mildly.

The Martian buildings---a better word might be structures---consisted of a jumbled array of spires and spheres, obelisks and triangles, pentagons and octagons, as well as other designs that could only be called abstract. The structures covered every square meter of available space, every shelf and outcropping and mesa and cliff top. All of which were linked by walkways and spans and ramps and avenues, some arching high, others curling low, and crisscrossing over and under each other in no perceivable pattern. The structures and the thoroughfares alike were composed of basalt.

KLL-12 had been briefed on what to expect prior to leaving Earth, thanks to Captain Archard Rahn's intel, but the spectacle still dazzled him.

Everywhere, there were Martians. Thousands upon thousands, of various forms and hues, going about their routines as humans in any city on Earth would do. Most were the small reddish variety, the crabs. Mixed among them, conspicuous by their size, were the huge blue warriors. Also conspicuous were far fewer green and brown.

Even with his genetically enhanced eyesight, KLL-12 saw no sign of a yellow one.

KLL-13 veered over to fly alongside him. "I don't see any leaders. How will we find a yellow critter in all of that?"

"Critter?" KLL-12 said.

"A human colloquialism. I like it. It fits."

"If you say so." KLL-12 couldn't care less. "We'll have to keep looking until we spot one."

"We don't have forever," KLL-13 said. "We're bound to be noticed sooner or later."

Sooner, it turned out. A red crab on an archway raised its eye stalks in their direction, and within moments, every Martian within sight stopped in their tracks and did the same.

"They know we're here," KLL-13 needlessly said.

"Then let's get to it."

KLL-12 swooped toward an edifice taller and more imposing than the rest on the theory that Martian leaders, like their Earth counterparts, enjoyed the trappings that came with power and prestige.

KLL-13 was scanning the space above them. "The flyers haven't caught up yet."

"Let's try to be gone by the time they do."

Gliding over the edifice, KLL-12 circled.

"What's your plan?" KLL-13 said. "Barge on in and grab the first yellow crustoid we come across?"

"Unless you have a better plan."

"I was kidding."

Below them, a giant blue warrior, the caste that resembled lobsters, used its powerful grippers to tear a piece of basalt from the causeway. Rearing onto its hind legs, it threw the basalt with incredible force but the piece fell short.

"We have a decision to make," KLL-12 said.

"We do?"

"Stay or leave."

"What are you talking about? We haven't completed our mission."

Fully aware that every second counted, KLL-12 banked and said, "Maybe we weren't intended to."

"You're making no sense."

"Look at all of them," KLL-12 said, with a nod at the alien metropolis. "We can't defeat that many. Our makers know that. Which means in their eyes we're expendable."

"All soldiers are," KLL-13 said. "You're quibbling. This is a snatch and grab. In and out. If we're killed, so be it." She gestured at the edifice. "Now quit wasting time."

"I don't trust our makers," KLL-12 said.

"You've made that tediously apparent," KLL-13 said. "But it's irrelevant. We can't break our conditioning. We have to follow orders whether we like them or not. So enough of this." With that, she tucked her membranes and dived.

As much as he would rather leave, KLL-12 did likewise. She was right. He had no choice. He had been given an order and he must obey. He must capture a yellow Martian or perish trying.

The tall structure bristled with Martians. More were rushing to the rooftop and terraces from within. Many waved their grippers as if in defiance, or maybe they were eager to close and do battle.

On the highest terrace were a half a dozen red crabs. KLL-13---boldly, brazenly, and typical of her---landed in their midst. They swarmed her, and for a few heartbeats, KLL-12 thought she would be overwhelmed. But no. With sweeps of her powerful arms, she cast half aside. One lunged at her face and she seized it by its forelimbs and tore the limbs off. Using them like clubs, she struck a second and a third, caving their carapaces.

By then, KLL-12 was at her side. He smashed a creature that leaped at KLL-13's back, drove his foot into another. Then, lifting a heavy slab of basalt that evidently served as the Martian equivalent of a bench, he reduced the last two to pulp.

Nearby, a dark entryway beckoned.

"Come on, big boy!" KLL-13 squealed and gained the entry in two bounds.

"Wait for me," KLL-12 said. By rights, he should be in front, since he was senior, but she hurtled on in. Annoyed, he hastened to catch up, only to come on a junction with three branching tunnels. He chose the one that slanted down and raced at full speed.

His subcutaneous commlink blared.

"I've found a yellow critter! I'm in a large chamber! Hurry! There are a lot of Martians!"

A crackling sound punctuated her transmission.

Alarmed that her rashness might get her killed, KLL-12 sped around a bend. The floor leveled and he burst into the chamber. Across the way stood a yellow Martian. Between it and him, there had to be a hundred creatures of all kinds.

And there, in the thick of them, battling for her life, was KLL-13.

23

There was no time for Captain Archard Rahn to climb into the RAM, no time for Lieutenant Burroughs and the rest of the strike team to reach the Thunderbolt.

The Martians flowing over the rise and those charging out of the tunnel would be on them before they could.

"Grenades!" Archard bellowed, feeding a frag into the launcher under the barrel of his ICW. He aimed at the tunnel roof, thinking that he might be able to bring it crashing down and not only kill a lot of Martians but bottleneck them inside.

The explosion blew Martians to bits and produced a cloud of dust but the roof stayed intact.

Private Everett spun toward the incoming tide and fired. His frag hit smack in the middle of the crustoid ranks but the blast barely slowed them.

They would soon be surrounded.

"Head for the Thunderbolt but keep formation!" Archard shouted. Their only hope lay in breaking through and taking flight.

Already, though, Martians were flowing around the aircraft in a torrent of scuttling limbs and waving eye stalks.

"We're cut off!" Sergeant Kline hollered.

"Fight!" Archard said grimly.

"Fight like hell!" Lieutenant Burroughs amended.

Fight they did. Frag grenades, incendiary grenades, autofire, they unleashed a hailstorm that cored and blistered the Martians, piling creatures in heaps. Yet despite of their most frantic efforts, the ring of crustaceans closed centimeter by centimeter.

A scream rent the bedlam.

A red Martian was clinging to Private Stratton with its four pairs of legs while its forelimbs tore at his helmet. Stratton smashed at the thing with his rifle stock but couldn't knock it off. Private Everett sprang to help and struck the Martian on its carapace but it had no more effect than beating on the shell of a crab with a stick.

Archard turned, knowing he shouldn't break formation but also knowing they couldn't afford to lose anyone. He managed a couple of strides when the inevitable happened.

A gripper shattered Private Stratton's helmet. The inrush of Martian atmosphere caused him to break out in convulsions. Unable to breathe, he gasped and heaved. He was dying of suffocation---and evaporation. Inside his body, the alveoli of his lungs were being boiled away, along with most of the water in his body. Not because of the surface temperature but because of the pressure differential.

"Close up!" Archard bawled, hoping the others heard him over the bedlam. There were only five of them now; five against a horde, and their ammunition wouldn't last forever.

The Martians poured in, mostly the red but now a couple of giant blue warriors were among them.

"God," Archard blurted. He had fought the blue warriors before. They were terribly tough, unbelievably tenacious. He had barely been able to hold his own in a RAM. In their EVA suits, the five of them stood no prayer at all.

Still, he was U.N.I.C., and troopers never gave up, never said die. He let loose with his last incendiary at one of the blue warriors and had the satisfaction of seeing it enveloped in chemical flames. But it kept coming.

"Tighten up!" Archard ordered. "Back to back!"

They pressed against each other, their final defiance in the face of imminent death. Any instant now, the ring of Martians would tear one or two of them down and the rest would be overrun.

A loud sound from above almost caused Archard to break his concentration and look up. It sounded like engines but that couldn't be, the only aircraft on Mars was the Thunderbolt. He triggered a burst into a leaping Martian, catching it in the underbelly and ripping it apart, swiveled, and fired into the "face" of another.

The engine sounds grew louder.

"Drop ships!" Sergeant Kline shouted over his commlink.

Archard focused his fire on the onrushing blue warrior. It was like shooting a tank. His armor-piercing rounds failed to penetrate deep enough to inflict a fatal wound.

The warrior was almost on them.

That was when the sky rained living forms---twenty-two of them---beings every bit as alien, in their way, as the Martians. The drops ships were fifteen meters above the ground but the tall figures that sprang from their bays leaped down without the aid of parachutes or paragliders. They simply jumped, a feat no human could duplicate and live.

Archard was both elated and confounded. The presence of drop ships meant the fleet from Earth had arrived. But they weren't due for a week to ten days. Why hadn't he been told they would arrive sooner? Did the governor know? He shook off the questions and drilled a red Martian that, inexplicably, froze in front of him.

Then Archard saw that all the Martians had stopped fighting and every last one had raised their eye stalks toward the drop ships and the reinforcements from Earth.

Those reinforcements appeared to be---amazingly enough--- reptilian. Covered in copper scales from their hairless heads to their pointed toenails, they gave the impression of being two-legged lizards. An impression dispelled when one of them landed with a surprisingly light thud between Archard and the blue warrior. Up close, human traits were apparent. They were hybrids, half-human and half-whatever the geneticists had mixed in the chemical brew.

The hybrid in front of Archard turned its head, fixed eyes with vertical pupils on him, and smiled.

"We're the BioMarines, Captain Rahn. General Augusto sent us to retrieve you."

Before Archard could recover his wits enough to reply, the ring of Martians came to life. In a rush, they renewed their assault. Except now the BioMarines had formed a protective circle around Archard and the other troopers.

To Archard's further surprise, the hybrids raised a fist in the air, and in unison gave voice to the U.N.I.C. rallying cry.

"Booyah!

"Booyah!" Sergeant Kline and Private Everett echoed. Archard, Burroughs, and Private Keller added their own. And the battle was joined.

24

General Constantine Augusto was pleased with himself. His fleet had arrived on the Red Planet and his forces were being deployed according to his plan. KLL-1 and the BioMarine unit had gone after Captain Rahn, and his secret stealth op was underway at Albor Tholus. An auspicious start to the war, if he did say so himself.

Bradbury's citizenry had turned out to greet their rescuers. Asimov Street, which ran from the main airlock into Dome One to the Admin Center, was lined with colonists waving and smiling and cheering.

Marching at the forefront of the U.N.I.C. contingent he had brought from Earth, his uniform immaculate, his helmet and medals gleaming, his boots spit-shined, General Augusto returned their waves and smiles. He could do without the adulation. He was a soldier, not a politician. But these people were scared and he needed to reassure them that their saviors had arrived. The Martians would soon learn the hard way that when you messed with Mother Earth, you called down the thunder and the lightning.

Slightly behind him, Major Fogarty, his aide-de-camp, remarked, "They're ecstatic to see you, sir."

"As well they should be."

"Do you think they'll feel the same once they've been told martial law is being imposed?" Major Fogarty said.

"Who cares how they feel?" General Augusto said. "We're here to kill Martians, not mollycoddle civilians."

A girl of ten or twelve ran out from her mother's side and held a flower up. "For you, General."

General Augusto smiled and accepted it. "Thank you, child."

Giggling, a hand over her mouth, she turned and ran back.

General Augusto handed the flower to Fogarty. "Dispose of this when we reach admin." He resumed waving and smiling.

"Do you mind my saying, sir," the major said, raising his voice to be heard. "Isn't protecting these people our primary directive?"

"Securing this planet for Earth is our mission," General Augusto said. "Everything else is subordinate to that."

"I just thought…" Major Fogarty began.

General Augusto silenced him with a glare. "Don't think, Major. Just do as I tell you. You're newly assigned as my aide, so I'll overlook your lapse this time."

"Yes, sir."

General Augusto waved to several women and keyed his commlink. "KLL-1, sitrep."

The answer was slow in coming, and when it did, crackled with static and the unmistakable sounds of pitched combat.

"We have located Rahn. Enemy engaged. More later. Out."

General Augusto had every confidence in the BioMarines. They were his babies, as it were. True, a scientist by the name of Greenspan developed the biogenetic techniques that made test-tube hybrids feasible. But it was he, Augusto, who recognized the military applications, and who persuaded those who controlled the purse strings at the U.N. to fund research into the creation of a hybrid unit.

Now here he was, on Mars, with a squad of BioMarines, about to demonstrate to two worlds that they were the ultimate in warfare.

Awash in pride, General Augusto paused to look back at his troopers and the column of tanks that had come through the airlock. The first of the new RAM's he had brought was just emerging. It was a shame the airlocks cycled so slowly but slow and safe was preferable to quick and dead.

"General Augusto! I say! General Augusto!"

Reminding himself to be civil, General Augusto turned. Hurrying toward him were Governor Blanchard and a striking blonde woman in a lab coat. "We were to meet in your office, Governor," Augusto reminded him.

"I'm sorry. It couldn't wait," Blanchard said and motioned at the woman. "This is Dr. Katla Dkany…"

General Augusto remembered her name from the reports he had read. He held out his hand. "You're one of the few survivors from the other colonies, yes? A pleasure to meet you."

"There's no time for pleasantries, General," the woman said. "I made the governor bring me. You need to be told."

"We don't have any proof," Blanchard said. "Just her word."

"Word about what?" Governor Augusto said in some annoyance.

"The Martians," Dr. Dkany said. "They're inside the domes."

25

The strangest sensation came over KLL-12 there in the large chamber in the bizarre Martian edifice. A sensation he had never experienced. A feeling, or better yet, a compulsion that came over him so swiftly, he was in motion before he realized what he was doing.

The cause of the compulsion was KLL-13. The sight of her battling with all her considerable might against a nigh-overwhelming number of Martians filled KLL-12 with fury. Why, he couldn't say. All he knew was that when she started to go down under the crustoid onslaught, he bounded into their midst---and went berserk.

KLL-12 prided himself on his supreme self-control. He never, ever, let his emotions get the better of him. They were the human part of his genetic makeup, and he had an extremely low opinion of everything human. Nonetheless, in this particular instant he let his emotions out, and it was like a dam bursting. Rage, potent, fiery hot, boiled in his veins.

KLL-12 wreaked havoc with uninhibited abandon. He rent legs. He ripped off forelimbs. He crushed carapaces. He swung and punched and kicked and smashed with a savagery even the Martians couldn't match. Within moments, he swept them from around KLL-13 and pulled her to her feet.

She looked at him in astonishment, her face and body bleeding in multiple spots.

"Fight!" KLL-12 cried, and suited his actions to his command. He tore into the Martians, a whirlwind in a wheat field, ripping and breaking and destroying his way toward their yellow leader.

Ever the vocal one, KLL-13 uttered a piercing yip of pure joy and joined in, her own control cast to the Martian winds.

Most of their foes were the reddish-pink variety. A few were brown. They went down easy. A blue warrior was trying to make it through the press but there were too many red crabs in the way.

Seizing one of the latter by its legs, KLL-12 employed it like a scythe, swinging it in great arcs that knocked others aside or fractured their limbs and bodies. He sent a last couple tumbling, cast his makeshift weapon aside, and reached the yellow leader.

Three meters high and a meter long, they were different than the rest in that they possessed two sets of three legs instead of two sets of four. They had the same forelimbs, and the same multifaceted eyes at the ends of long stalks that could be retracted into recesses in their large, bowl-shaped heads.

This one showed no fear as KLL-12 seized hold. To his surprise, it didn't resist as he hauled it toward the tunnel through which they had entered. All it did was turn its obscenely large head in the direction of the blue warrior.

Something happened. KLL-12 couldn't say what, but suddenly the giant blue Martian exploded into motion, propelling its lobster-shaped bulk toward him like an express train.

"Take this thing," KLL-12 shouted, shoving the yellow Martian at KLL-13. "Get out of here."

The red Martians were scuttling from the blue creature's path, even those with their backs to it.

How they could know it was behind them when they weren't looking that way was a mystery.

Then the warrior was on him, its large grippers spread wide. Leaping high, KLL-12 avoided them. At the apex of his jump, he performed a somersault and came down on top of the blue creature's back. As he landed, he drove his claw-tipped fingers as deep into the carapace as they would go. Before the Martian could divine his intent, he ripped its carapace open.

A serrated gripper streaked at KLL-12's head.

Ducking, he wrenched harder, peeling back a section of carapace as if it were the skin of an orange. The creature's other gripper whipped at his chest, and he flattened. Quickly, he drove his claws deeper into its flesh. The sensation was akin plunging his hand into mud; cool and clammy and sticky. He groped wildly, seeking an organ, any organ. Supposedly, the Martians had hearts and circulatory systems and other internal parts that corresponded to their crustacean counterparts on Earth.

Luck was with him. KLL-12's splayed fingers made contact with what felt like a pulpy sac. Gripping tight, he ripped whatever-it-was out of the creature's body.

The blue warrior broke into convulsions.

Coiling, KLL-12 vaulted clear over the smaller Martians and came down not two meters from the tunnel.

KLL-13 was waiting, the yellow leader clasped like a giant doll under her arm. Oddly, the creature still wasn't offering any resistance.

"I told you to go!" KLL-12 exclaimed.

"Not without you."

"Go, damn you!" KLL-12 bellowed.

Smiling, she did.

KLL-12 at her heels, they retraced their route to the topmost level. Reaching the terrace, they each took hold of the yellow leader forelimbs. Then, their free arms outspread and their membranes taut, they launched themselves from the terrace.

Their escape route had been worked out in advance. Once again, thanks to Captain Rahn's intel, they knew there was a large tunnel on the west wall of the cavern, a passage that would eventually take them up to the outside world. All they had to do was reach it.

Below them, on arches and ramps and rooftops, Martians watched, their eye stalks immobile.

"I said it before and I'll say it again," KLL-13 said. "Spooky damn things."

"You took a big risk back there," KLL-12 said.

"We caught one, didn't we?" KLL-13 said. "Speaking of which, why isn't this thing fighting us?"

"I don't know."

"I don't like it."

KLL-12 scanned their vicinity for flyers. "Stay focused. We have a long ways to go."

Bending her head, KLL-13 looked over at him and became uncharacteristically serious. "Thanks for the save."

"It was nothing," KLL-12 said, and his ears grew warm.

"I didn't know you cared," KLL-13 said with a grin.

"Don't make more of it than there was. You're essential to the mission, is all."

"Uh-huh."

They passed over an archway crammed with Martians, all of which raised their grippers in unison.

"Did you see that?" KLL-13 said. "I'm beginning to think they have some kind of telepathy."

"Let's hope not or we might not make it out of here alive."

26

Captain Archard Rahn was in awe. The previous times he fought the Martians, he was lucky to survive. They were tough as anything, brutal as could be, biological killing machines.

But now the U.N.I.C. had killing machines of their own.

The BioMarines met the assault with a ruthlessness that was astounding to witness. Not only did they possess lightning reflexes the equal of the Martians, but their superhuman strength also matched that of their adversaries, enabling them to tear the Martians limb from limb and crush Martian carapaces as if the shells were so much plastic.

Moving so fast it was difficult to follow, the BioMarines smashed and rent in an orgy of destruction. It helped that they fought as a synchronous whole, each supporting the other, coordinating their tactics in totality.

The Martians tried to bring them down. In ranks they drove at the hybrids, and in ranks they were slaughtered.

A blue warrior threw itself into the fray and was met by three BioMarines simultaneously. One leaped onto its back, another attacked its legs, the third slammed a scale-covered fist wrist-deep into its head.

The blue warrior buckled in its tracks.

Archard had never imagined they could be defeated so quickly. His appreciation was cut short as he joined in, he and his ops team adding their firepower to the melee. Shooting in three-round bursts to conserve ammo, he dropped Martians where he could, careful not to hit his new allies.

The battle ended with impossible swiftness.

The Martians broke it off. Hundreds were dead or dying when the rest stopped fighting and---as one---streamed into the tunnel.

There were a few last shots from Private Everett and Private Keller. Then silence fell save for the heavy breathing of the troopers and the scritching and scratching of weakly thrashing Martians.

"Kicked their asses," a female BioWarrior said, and she and the others raised their gore-smeared fists in a chorus of, "Booyah!"

The BioMarine who had spoken to Archard earlier turned. From head to feet, his copper-hued body was splattered with Martian blood. Showing no fatigue whatsoever, he performed a snappy salute. "KLL-1, at your service, Captain Rahn."

"I don't quite know what to say," Archard wearily admitted.

"Your ordeal is over," KLL-1 said. "We're under orders from General Augusto to escort you and your strike team to Bradbury."

"I'll fly there in the RAM," Archard said, nodding toward the battlesuit.

"That won't be necessary, sir," KLL-1 said. "Lieutenant Burroughs is to take it back. You're to be ferried in the Thunderbolt." He paused. "The general's orders, sir."

"In that case," Archard said, although it galled him being treated so summarily.

Burroughs had been listening and remarked jokingly, "Don't worry, sir. I'll get it back in one piece."

She stared up at the hybrid. "But who will fly the Thunderbolt?"

"KLL-9," KLL-1 said, indicating a female hybrid. "She is rated for most types of aircraft."

"If you don't mind my asking," Lieutenant Burroughs said, "how do you breathe without an EVA suit? You're from Earth, like us."

"I would enjoy discussing our biological capabilities with you sometime, Lieutenant," KLL-1 said. "But the general wants the captain returned ASAP. We must depart immediately." He motioned toward the Thunderbolt. Beyond it, drop ships were settling to the ground to disgorge troopers and tanks. "After you, Captain Rahn."

Archard's resentment mounted. They were treating him almost like a prisoner. Nevertheless, he slung his ICW, nodded at the rest of his team, and trudged toward the Thunderbolt. "The general went to all this trouble just for me?"

KLL-1 strode beside him, taking small steps to match his pace. On his other side was another BioMarine, with four more behind.

"And to bring back those with you," KLL-1 said.

"We failed in our mission," Archard said bitterly. "We were supposed to capture a Martian leader."

"Lieutenant Burroughs and the others were, not you, personally, sir," KLL-1 said.

"Ah," Archard said. "Am I to take it the general is mad at me for violating his orders?"

"You'll need to take that up with him," KLL-1 said. "But take heart in that as we speak, a stealth op by two BioMarines may have succeeded where you didn't."

"How's that again?"

"General Augusto sent two of our unit into Albor Tholus to take a yellow leader prisoner. The latest satlink indicates they have done so and emerged safely from the volcano."

"Wait a minute," Archard said. "Are you saying Lieutenant Burroughs and her people were sent on a diversionary mission?"

"Not at all, sir," KLL-1 said. "The general believes simultaneous ops increase the prospect of success."

"You sound as if you know him really well," Archard said.

"I flatter myself that I do, sir, yes," KLL-1 said. He gestured at the other BioMarines. "We are his personal strike team and answer only to him."

"How nice," Archard said.

"Is something wrong, sir?"

"A whole lot of things," Archard said. "We're in the middle of a war."

"For which we were specifically bred," KLL-1 said, smiling. "As you humans would say, life doesn't get any better than this."

Archard begged to differ, but didn't.

27

Colonel Vasin wasn't a happy soldier. He liked giving orders more than he liked being ordered around, and he definitely didn't like being ordered to personally lead a squad of troopers down to the incinerator room in the Science Center to verify Dr. Katla Dkany's claim of seeing Martians.

Vasin was sure he was on a goose chase. Yes, the other two colonies had been attacked from below and overrun. But he'd taken steps to prevent the same catastrophe from occurring at Bradbury. For starters, he'd instructed his tech people to install motion sensors in every maintenance tunnel and conduit. He had cameras placed at strategic points. He'd also directed that listening posts be set up under each dome and be monitored twenty-four-seven.

Vasin was confident the Martians hadn't penetrated his protective net. Dr. Dkany suspected the creatures were coming in through the water pipes, but to do that, they'd have to pass through various filtration systems and trigger all sorts of alarms.

"Almost there, sir," Sergeant Herbert said.

Colonel Vasin glanced at the elevator panel. "Lock and load, just in case."

"Yes, sir." Herbert gestured at the four troopers, who checked the magazines in their ICW's.

Colonel Vasin had a thought. "On the remote chance the good doctor is right, no one is to use frags down here. Understood?" He could just see a main water pipe take a hit, and the lower levels flooding.

"What about armor-piercing round, sir?" Sergeant Herbert asked.

"Better play it safe."

"Yes, sir." Sergeant Herbert sounded dubious. "You heard the colonel, men. Standard ammo."

The door pinged and Colonel Vasin emerged and strode to the incinerator room. The door was shut. He was about to open it when Sergeant Herbert said, "In case she is right, sir, maybe we should go first."

Vasin stepped to one side. He was unarmed except for a pistol, so they wouldn't think less of him for playing it safe.

"On me," Sergeant Herbert said to his men. Throwing the door wide, he barreled in. The rest followed suit.

Colonel Vasin waited until he heard, "All clear." The first thing he noticed was a smear of blood on the floor. No body, though, and no sign of Martians anywhere. "Anything?" "Negative, sir."

The room appeared deserted.

Colonel Vasin headed for the main water pipe. The hatch that Dr. Dkany claimed was open was now closed. He examined it and found a few scratch marks that could have been made by a tool as readily as claws. "Seems to have been a waste of our time." As he had suspected would be the case.

"What about the blood, sir?"

"A worker hurt themself," Colonel Vasin guessed. Although, now that he examined it more closely, it was an awful lot of blood. "When we're topside, get on the horn to the hospital. Find out if they've admitted anyone today."

"Will do, sir."

Colonel Vasin supposed he shouldn't blame Dr. Dkany for the false alarm. After what she went through, she was entitled to frayed nerves. He didn't realize he'd said it out loud until Sergeant Herbert responded.

"What about the other witness, sir? Do we discount both of them?"

"The other one didn't get as good a look," Colonel Vasin said. "Could be she imagined it. Her fear was fed by Dkany's."

"Could be," Sergeant Herbert said.

"In any event, I need to report to the general," Vasin said, and did so, keeping it short and sweet, ending with, "There are no signs of any hostiles, sir."

"Good. Report back ASAP."

"Yes, sir." "Vasin motioned at the others. "Let's go."

They were halfway to the door when a young trooper called out, "Motion readings, sir!"

"Where?" Sergeant Herbert barked.

The young trooper was tweaking his scanner. "I'm not sure, Sarge. It was there and it was gone."

Colonel Vasin activated his helmet holo display and amped the gain on his own sensors. The only movement he picked up was their own. He switched to infrared and swept the incinerator room. The only heat sigs were theirs. "A glitch," he guessed.

"I swear there was something, sir," the young trooper insisted.

"Could you at least tell which direction?" Sergeant Herbert said.

"Not really, Sarge. Sorry."

Colonel Vasin looked right and left and then straight up. He was about to remark that they were wasting their time but he froze with his mouth half-open.

Directly overhead, jutting from over the pipes and ducts that honeycombed the ceiling, were scores of long stalks capped by compound eyes.

Martian eyes.

Vasin went to shout a warning, to tell his men that the creatures were on top of the pipes. He was too late. The Martians launched themselves from their perches.

Sergeant Herbert managed to get off a burst but then he and the others were buried under the weight of a rain of crustaceans.

Bleating in dismay, Colonel Vasin ran for the door. He managed a couple of steps when it felt as if the entire weight of the Red Planet slammed onto his shoulders and brought him crashing down. His arms and legs were pinned, and before he could use his commlink, his helmet was ripped from his head.

Vasin struggled to break free. His vision was blocked by a forest of red limbs and the bottoms of carapaces.

A pair of eye stalks lowered and the Martian's eyes bored into his.

Panic welled as a pair of grippers seized him by the head. Vasin remembered Captain Rahn and Dr. Dkany saying the Martians often took the heads of those they slew.

"Please, no," Colonel Vasin gasped.

He experienced a terrible tearing sensation, and a flood of agony thankfully brief. Strangely, he found himself looking down at his own body and saw his arms and legs being ripped off. His body, spraying blood, bucked wildly.

A series of colors enveloped him. The deepest black, a translucent gray, and finally, a vivid green that sucked him into oblivion.

28

General Constantine Augusto was immensely pleased. His double-pronged stratagem to capture a Martian leader had been successful. Captain Archard Rahn, despite defying orders, would soon arrive back at Bradbury. His troopers and tanks were being deployed in a defensive perimeter outside the colony, and within.

General Augusto smiled. Just let the Martians try something. He would repel anything they threw at him.

"What did Colonel Vasin have to say?" a female voice intruded on his reverie.

General Augusto looked up in annoyance. He had commandeered the governor's office for the interim, and across the desk sat Dr. Katla Dkany, anxiously tapping her fingers on the arm of her chair. "He reported all is well. You need not remain."

"He was lying."

"Vasin is a career soldier, madam, and not in the habit of deceiving his superiors."

"I tell you I saw Martians."

"Perhaps you only think you did."

"General, I want---" she angrily began.

Holding up a hand to stop her, General Augusto stood. He had been courteous long enough. "Enough. I appreciate your concern. You have to agree I've been reasonable. I sent the colonel to investigate. But now the matter is settled." Going around the desk, he went to place a hand on her shoulder but changed his mind when she glanced at him sharply. "Besides, don't you have a child who needs looking after?"

"Piotr Zabinski," Katla said. "His parents were killed at New Meridian and I've taken him under my wing. My friend, Trisna Sahir, is watching him."

"The other survivor from the earlier attacks?"

Dr. Dkany nodded. "Her and her daughter."

"You should go to them," General Augusto said. He had infinitely more important matters to attend to. Indicating the door, he said, "If I need to get in touch, I know where to find you."

She reluctantly rose. "I still think Colonel Vasin is mistaken. Please keep searching."

"Have no fear on that score," General Augusto assured her. He ushered her out, then crooked a finger at Major Fogarty, who was waiting.

"Sir?"

"Status report."

"The Thunderbolt is landing as we speak. A drop ship has been sent to pick up KLL-12 and 13 and the Martian."

"How much trouble has it given them?" General Augusto was curious to learn.

"They report it has been oddly docile," Major Fogarty said. "It's made no attempt to break its restraints."

"These creatures aren't as formidable as Captain Rahn and Dr. Dkany made them out to be."

"They did destroy two colonies," Major Fogarty said, quickly adding, "Sir."

"Only because they caught both colonies off-guard," General Augusto said. "Neither were prepared, as we are. Neither had the troops and armaments we do." He moved to a window and gazed out over the buildings and streets protected by the golden dome.

"Our outer emplacements are almost complete," the major reported. "Am I to infer our mission on Mars will be primarily defensive, sir?"

"Hardly. There's an old Earth adage that the best defense is a good offense. I'd go that one better. The best defense is a devastating offense. Once our perimeter is secure, I intend to carry the fight to the Martians." Augusto made sure none of their subordinates were in earshot and quietly said, "Have the nukes been brought down?"

Major Fogarty nodded and said equally quietly, "At the moment, they are stored in Sublevel Four at U.N.I.C. headquarters." He paused. "I still can't believe the secretary-general gave his consent to use them on the Martians."

"Who says he did?" General Augusto said, and almost laughed when Fogarty paled.

"Sir? Surely you're not suggesting..."

"I'm saying I will do whatever is necessary," General Augusto said. "Mars is as much ours now as it is theirs. We have every right to be here. We're the superior culture, after all. And what happens when a superior civilization encounters an inferior one?" He didn't wait for a reply. "The inferior is absorbed or eliminated. And we certainly can't absorb the Martians. Hell, we can't even communicate with them. Our only recourse is to wipe them out."

"What will the governments of Earth say?"

General Augusto squared his shoulders. "They will thank us for our foresight and courage in dealing with the enemy the only way we could."

"It sounds to me as if you have the war all planned out, sir," Major Fogarty said.

"Did you expect any less?" General Augusto said. "Once the Martian leader is in maximum security, we'll send an ultimatum to the Martians. Surrender or we'll drop a nuke down Albor Tholus."

Major Fogarty couldn't hide his confusion. "But you just said we have no way to communicate with them. They won't be able to respond."

"Isn't that a shame?" General Augusto said, and laughed.

29

Bradbury's Visitor Center was exactly like the Visitor Centers at Wellsville and New Meridian. As well it should be, since all three were constructed from the same modules and outfitted and decorated according to the same U.N. guidelines. The official document was called The United Nations Mars Protocols, with regulations and rules covering every aspect of life on the Red Planet.

Dr. Katla Dkany was sick of staying there. The small rooms, the antiseptic décor, the sameness, were not to her liking. The admin people kept promising she would soon have her own place but it was taking forever.

Given the day she was having, Katla wasn't in the best of moods as she took the elevator to the second floor. Her room was 212 but she stopped at 211 and knocked. She heard giggles, and a woman with a clipped accent said, "Hold on. Someone is at the door."

Trisna Sahir's long black hair was perfectly in place, her shift immaculate. Fastidious by nature, she was as devoted to her appearance as she was to being Hindu. "Katla!" she said with delight, and impulsively hugged her. "Behulah! Piotr! Look who is home."

The two children, who were playing cards on the floor, leaped up.

Behulah Sahir was the spitting image of her mother. Normally quiet and shy, she had taken to regarding Katla as a sort of "aunt." The girl, too, gave her a hug.

Piotr Zabinski hung back. Not quite eleven years old, he had matured considerably since the deaths of his mother and father.

"Don't I get a hug from you?" Katla said.

Awkwardly, self-consciously, Piotr flung an arm around her waist and quickly stepped back.

"You call that a hug?"

The boy shrugged. "I don't want to cling like I did before."

"You had cause. You'd just lost your parents," Katla said without thinking, and regretted it. The sadness his face mirrored was heart-wrenching. Pulling him to her, she hugged him, then tousled his hair. "How about you thank Trisna for letting you hang out here while I was at work, and we go to our place and eat supper?"

"No need to go," Trisna said. "I made curry and have rice warming on the stove. Please. Stay. There are things we must talk about, you and I."

Katla recognized her friend's tone. Something had happened. Something that upset Trisna but which she didn't want to discuss in front of the children. "Sure."

Katla took out her phone, checked for a message from Archard, and when she didn't find one, tapped a text that she was at Trisna's.

Over at the sink, her friend had begun slicing bread. "No word from that handsome man of yours?"

"Who knows what they have him doing?" Katla said glumly. She dearly yearned for them to be allowed to return to Earth where they could commence a new life, free of the constant fear that gnawed at her every waking moment.

"Kids, continue with your game," Trisna cheerfully told the children. When they did, she leaned toward Katla and lowered her voice. "Have you heard the rumors?"

"Which?" Katla said.

"The Martians are loose in Bradbury," Trisna whispered. "I heard it from the lobby clerk who heard it from her mother who got it straight from the mouth of a man who knows someone who does maintenance work at the Administration Center."

"They are loose," Katla said.

"What?" Trisna stopped slicing. "You know this for a fact? How?"

"I saw them."

Startled, Trisna recoiled, the knife slipping from her fingers. The sound of it striking the floor was like the crack of a shot. The kids looked over and Behulah laughed.

"You are a butterfingers, Mother."

"Play your game," Trisna said. Scooping the knife up, she set it on the counter. "Haven't you told anyone? The last newscast made no mention of it."

"I went to General Augusto personally," Katla said. "He sent troopers to where I saw the Martians but they didn't find any."

"So now he doubts your word?"

"Pretty much," Katla said.

Trisna bowed her head and trembled. "I refuse to live through this again. I've had enough stupidity to last me a lifetime." She gripped Katla's sleeve. "What do we do?"

"I've been thinking," Katla said quietly. "I have an idea. I want to run it by Archard and get his input before I say anything."

"Tell me," Trisna said.

Katla glanced at the kids to be sure they weren't listening. "Where's the one place we would be safe if Bradbury is attacked?"

"There is no safe haven," Trisna said. "The entire planet is under Martian control."

"What about off-planet?"

"Excuse me?"

Katla pointed straight up. "The fleet in orbit. The one place the Martian's can't get to. So what if we commandeer a drop ship and fly up to one of the transports?"

"Commandeer?" Trisna said, aghast. "You mean *steal*?"

"It's our only hope," Katla said. "And those spaceships won't be up there forever. They'll be returning to Earth. We need to be on board when they do."

"Oh, Katla," Trisna said. "Your idea could get us in a lot of trouble."

"It beats being dead."

30

The Thunderbolt streaked out of the Martian sky and hovered over the hangar complex near Dome One. From his seat behind the pilot's chair, Captain Archard Rahn had a bird's-eye view of the activity taking place.

The entire colony was being fortified. Laser and microwave emplacements ringed the domes. Tanks were in camouflaged positions outside and roved the streets within. Hundreds of troopers in EVA suits were digging in, while hundreds more patrolled the streets.

The drop ships were lined up on the flight concourse. Some were being retrofitted with machine guns and missiles as an additional defense.

Archard had to hand it to General Augusto. The man had covered every contingency. It would take a million Martians to break through the perimeter.

The trouble was, Archard suspected there were many millions.

He sat up as the Thunderbolt descended to its landing pad near the hangar, the ground crew rushing to meet it.

"And we're down, people," KLL-9 announced. She had handled the craft with supreme finesse.

The entire flight, KLL-1 had stood with his hands clasped behind his back in the parade rest position, directly behind Archard. Now he stirred, a statue coming to life. "My orders are to escort you to the general, Captain."

"Wonder if I'll be demoted?" Archard said, only partly in jest.

"I'm sure I wouldn't know," KLL-1 said. "After you, if you please."

Archard sealed his EVA helmet, slung his ICW, and punched the code for the airlock. He was mildly surprised they hadn't taken his weapon, but then, he hadn't been formally charged with anything yet.

Entering the airlock, he moved to one side to make room for KLL-1, who had to duck to fit. The inner door closed and the outer door cycled.

KLL-1 had a finger to his temple and appeared to be listening to his commlink. "Good news, Captain. KLL-12 and KLL-13 have arrived with their prisoner. We're to report to U.N.I.C. headquarters where General Augusto will oversee the interrogation."

The outer door opened and again the BioMarine said, "After you, Captain."

Archard had the impression he was under guard. He headed for the hangar, expecting they would use the access tunnel into Dome One.

"The general has requested that we expedite our arrival," KLL-1 said. "With your permission?"

Before Archard could ask what the hybrid intended, he felt its large hands slide under his arms from behind and the next moment he was bodily lifted a good twenty meters into the air. "What the---!" he blurted.

"Relax, Captain," KLL-1 said. "I have you."

The BioMarine had jumped. At the apex of his leap, he spread his elbows wide to either side and ribbed membranes popped out of recessed grooves under his arms.

"Wings?" Archard exclaimed.

"Not quite," KLL-1 said. Tilting his body, he soared toward the airlock to Dome One.

Archard was astounded. "You're gliding like a bird."

"So to speak," KLL-1 said, his eerie eyes flicking over the bustle below. "One of the many biological improvements genetically encoded into us."

"What else can you do that we can't?"

"Many things," KLL-1 said, and enigmatically left it at that.

The golden dome seemed to rush up to meet them. KLL-1 titled again, and just-like-that, his membranes slowed them, enabling him to alight as gently as the proverbial feather.

"You BioMarines are something else," Archard complimented him.

"We are as we were created to be. The first line of defense in the human initiative to claim the solar system as its own."

"The solar system?" Archard said, and laughed. "Aren't you getting ahead of yourself?"

"Not according to General Augusto."

The comment gave Archard something to think about as they negotiated the airlock and climbed into the bay of a waiting tank. The sergeant driving had little to say and they covered the three blocks to H.Q. listening to a news feed proclaiming that General Augusto was the colony's new commander-in-chief, and his first official act had been to impose martial law.

"He doesn't waste any time," Archard said.

Hunched over in a corner, KLL-1 smiled. "The general? No, he doesn't. He likes to say he is a doer, not a talker. His motto is think ahead but act now."

"Never heard that one," Archard said.

"The general is a unique human."

"You say that fondly," Archard observed.

"Why wouldn't I?" KLL-1 responded. "Do not let my appearance deceive you. We have feelings, the same as you." He paused. "Well, most of us, and to varying degrees."

U.N.I.C. headquarters was a beehive. Officers and troopers were coming and going. The motor pool was busy with vehicles. Drones winged off and returned.

No sooner did Archard enter the building than General Augusto, trailed by officers and staff, hustled up. Archard barely had time to salute before the general seized him by the shoulders.

"Captain Rahn! At last we meet in person." General Augusto thrust out his hand.

Baffled by his reception, Archard shook. "General, sir. I was under the impression I was in hot water."

"Forget that for now," General Augusto said. "Your timing is perfect. I want you to come with me and be part of my team." Wheeling, he strode off.

Quickly falling into step, Archard said, "What exactly are we doing, sir?"

General Augusto beamed. "We're about to interrogate the Martian we caught. You get to listen to it squeal."

31

Private Everett was looking forward to a few hours off. It was the least the U.N.I.C. could offer after the ordeal he and the others had been through. As he wearily trudged down the hall to the dorm at H.Q., he remarked, "I don't know about you, but a beer or three is just what my throat needs."

"We're still on duty," Private Keller tiredly reminded him.

"My throat doesn't care," Everett said. It felt as if he had sweated out every drop of water in his body. Not only that, he was hungry enough to eat a blue Martian, raw.

"Hold on, there, you two!"

Everett stopped and turned, and groaned.

Sergeant Kline, his EVA suit still spattered with gore from their battle, had the look of someone who bore bad news.

"Whatever it is, Sarge," Everett said, "we don't want any."

Private Keller leaned her back to the wall and sagged. "We're beat, Sarge."

"Makes three of us," Kline said. "But we're to report to Captain Ferris on the perimeter defense detail." He held up a hand. "Before you say anything, I told the major that after what we went through, it's not fair to send us right back out. He said he understood and he's sorry but there's no down time for anyone right now."

"Well, hell," Everett said.

"We're to refill our air tanks and ammo-up and report within thirty minutes," Sergeant Kline told them.

"Damn Martians," Private Keller said.

It took closer to forty-five. They had to wait in line for their ammo and grenades, and wait again at the airlock.

Everett rarely let himself get down in the dumps but he was bummed by the decision to send them back out. Normally, the U.N.I.C. didn't treat its troopers so shabbily.

Captain Ferris, it turned out, had been assigned to defend a trench dug between a pair of maser emplacements. She was tall and lanky and wore her corn-colored hair in a crew. "Glad to have you," she said when Sergeant Kline reported to her. "There's only been four of us to cover a hundred meter area. Now we have seven."

Sergeant Kline swapped looks with Everett and Keller. "Stretching it a little thin, aren't we, sir?"

"Not my doing," Captain Ferris said. "The general is keeping a lot of troopers in reserve inside the domes."

Sergeant Kline gazed along the long line of masers, lasers, and ion cannons ringing the north dome. "He's big on firepower, I see."

"We have enough firepower to reduce any Martian army to cinders," Captain Ferris boasted.

"We hope," Everett said under his breath.

"I didn't quite catch that, Private," Captain Ferris said.

"Begging the captain's pardon," Everett said, "but the general hasn't seen what those critters are capable of. I have. And let me tell you. We're in for another ass-kicking if this is all the general has up his sleeve."

"Give General Augusto more credit," Captain Ferris said. "We have the drop ships. We have the BioMarines. We have the RAMs. We have spaceships in orbit that can lob nukes if they have to. There is no way in hell Bradbury will fall like Wellsville and New Meridian. This time, we're doing it right."

"Yes, sir," Everett said with more conviction than he felt. He had been at those two places, and if there was one thing he had learned, it was that the Martians were as tricky as they came.

Captain Ferris was about to say more but a trooper hurried up and snapped a salute.

"Ma'am! We're getting those readings again."

"Readings?" Sergeant Kline said.

"Come with me," Captain Ferris said.

Midway along the trench, a nook had been excavated for an augmented sensor unit and the trooper operating it. State of the art, the equipment was ten times more sensitive to motion and heat and other elements than the sensors in their EVA suits.

"What are you picking up, Rictor?" Captain Ferris asked the corporal at the controls.

"More seismic activity, sir," Rictor said. "Faint, but it's there."

"Your best guess as to the cause?"

"It could be nothing but tremors," Rictor said. "Mars has them now and then."

Everett couldn't keep quiet. "Pardon me again, Captain. But you do know that the Martians live underground? And that they move through dirt as easy and you and me walk around up here?"

"You're saying it's them?"

"Could well be, yes, ma'am."

Captain Ferris gnawed at her lower lip, then said, "Even so. So long as they stay down deep, we don't have anything to worry about."

"From your mouth to God's ears," Everett said.

32

The BioMarines were gathered in a meeting room on sublevel one of U.N.I.C. headquarters. After their return from pulling Captain Archard Rahn and his people out of the proverbial fire, General Augusto had told them to stand down for a while and await new orders.

KLL-1 stood at the head of the long table and regarded his fellow hybrids with satisfaction. "We performed well today. You should all be proud."

"Should we?" KLL-12 said from the other end of the table.

"You weren't with us," KLL-1 said. "We exceeded our creators' expectations. We took out a swarm of Martians without a single loss."

"Must have made the humans happy," KLL-12 said.

KLL-1 leaned on the table and his vertical pupils narrowed. "Is there a problem?"

"Don't mind grumpy," KLL-13 said. "He's not happy unless he's complaining."

Several of the others grinned.

Sweeping them with a look of annoyance, KLL-12 said, "None of you get it, do you? You've all been brainwashed by our makers."

"Explain yourself," KLL-1 said.

KLL-12 tapped the table a few times, then nodded. "Very well. I'll probably be wasting my breath, but here goes." He paused. "No, I wasn't with you. I didn't see you slaughter the Martians. But you weren't with KLL-13 and me, either. You didn't penetrate the Martian underground. You didn't see one of the cities with your own eyes."

"What is your point?" KLL-21 said.

"The city was enormous. There were tens of thousands of Martians of all kinds. KLL-13 and I were fortunate to make it out alive."

The other BioMarines were interested now and listening intently.

"And that was just one city. Who knows how many there are? Given the size of the planet, there could be hundreds. Perhaps thousands." KLL-12 was warming to his topic and stood. "Think about that. We could be talking *millions* of Martians. And there are only twenty-four of us."

KLL-12 stopped to let that sink in, then stared hard at KLL-1. "I know what you're going to say. We're not fighting them alone. We're allied with the humans, and they---"

"We are not their allies," KLL-1 interrupted. "We are soldiers under their command."

"What gives them the right to tell us what to do?" KLL-12 said.

"They created us," KLL-1 said.

"And programmed us so we can't refuse a direct order," KLL-12 said. "We're not soldiers. We've slaves."

"Not that again," KLL-13 sighed.

"Mock me all you want," KLL-12 said, "but take heed of my warning. If I'm right and there are more Martians than anyone believes, the twenty-four of us aren't enough to stop them. For that matter, the entire army General Augusto has deployed will not be enough."

"You don't know that," KLL-1 said. "The humans aren't fools. They have planned for every contingency."

"Based on the parameters of their reasoning," KLL-12 said. "But they are dealing with an unknown, new species whose abilities and limits have not been fully assessed. Which means there are contingencies the humans haven't planned for because they don't realize they exist."

"Listen to the big brain," KLL-13 teased, but none of the others laughed.

KLL-12 wasn't done. "The humans designed us to be their ultimate weapons. But even ultimate weapons have their limits."

"Again, you are indulging in speculation," KLL-1 said.

"I'm also suggesting we should rethink our part in the scheme of things. Instead of relying on the humans, we should start to work things out for ourselves."

"We are soldiers. We do as we are told," KLL-1 said. "It is our purpose. Our life."

Fully half the BioMarines gave voice to a, "Booyah!"

"Yes, that's the purpose we were created for," KLL-12 said. "But I, for one, have no wish to die. All I ask is that you consider what I've said. And if events prove our trust in the humans is misguided, that you give thought to doing whatever is necessary to ensure our own survival."

KLL-1 put a finger to his temple and motioned for silence as he listened to his subcutaneous commlink. "It's the general. We're to report to the brig on sublevel ten. The interrogation is about to begin." He straightened and regarded KLL-12. "As for you and your malcontent attitude, so long as I'm in charge, we'll do exactly as we are ordered. We wouldn't exist if it weren't for the humans. We owe them to do whatever they ask of us."

"Even if they ask us to die?"

KLL-13 laughed. "Get over yourself, big boy. We're warriors, and we're at war. It's as simple as that."

Standing, she clapped him on the arm. "Now come on. Let's go to the interrogation."

"Do you think the humans will torture it?" K-4 wondered.

"I know I would," KLL-13 said. "What fun is war without a little sadism?"

33

The lowest level of the United National Interplanetary Command Headquarters included holding cells that were hardly ever used. Only the most psychologically fit troopers were sent to Mars. Breaches of discipline were rare.

With walls a meter thick and constructed of the same nigh-impervious alloy as the rest of the prefabricated modules, the holding cells were the most secure containment facility in the colony.

One of the cells had been cleared of its cot and stool and was totally bare. Electronically controlled shackles welded to a large frame had been placed against the rear wall. And there, held in place, was their prisoner. Its long forelimbs were shackled. So were its six legs.

Wire leads to a biological scanner had been attached to the Martian and several scientists were monitoring the hookups.

The yellow Martian's most notable feature was the enormous bowl-shaped carapace that crowned its body. The bowl shape and size suggested the creature possessed a brain of considerable intellect. At the moment, its long eye stalks were extended and its multifaceted eyes were fixed on General Constantine Augusto.

Captain Archard Rahn was distinctly uneasy. Over twenty people were crammed into the cell, and a pair of BioMarines stood guard at the door. But Archard had a sense that the Martian was only interested in the general. The creature must know Augusto was in charge. Perhaps by simple deduction, since the general was the only one barking orders. Or was it something more?

The head of the Science Center, Dr. Clarence Huffington, brought over an e-reader and showed it to Augusto.

"There's not much to report, I'm afraid, General. We haven't been able to take a blood sample. The thing's shell is too thick for our needles to penetrate."

General Augusto gave the readings a glance and thrust the e-reader at the scientist. "We've only just begun, Doctor. An hour from now we'll know a lot more." He turned to his aide, Major Fogarty. "Have a power saw and a drill brought down."

The major whisked out.

"Look at it," General Augusto said. Striding over, he placed his hands on his hips and glared up at its compound eyes. "If this thing thinks it can drive us from Mars, it has another think coming."

"We've tried communicating, with no result," Dr. Huffington said. "And yet..." He looked at the bowl-shaped brain and stopped.

"And yet what?" General Augusto prompted.

"Nothing," Dr. Huffington said. "Jitters, I suppose. I've never examined an alien life form before."

Archard cleared his throat. "If I may make an observation, sir?"

"That's why you're here," General Augusto said. "You're the only real expert we have on these things."

"I wouldn't go that far," Archard said. "But I did have the impression they communicate differently than we do."

"How so?"

"When I stumbled on their underground city, one of them spotted me. The moment it did, every last creature stopped what it was doing and turned and stared. It was as if they shared some sort of mental link."

"Telepathy?" Dr. Huffington said. "You're suggesting they can read our minds?"

Archard shrugged. "I don't know about ours but they appear to be able to read each other's."

"That's ridiculous," General Augusto said.

Dr. Huffington knit his brow. "I wouldn't be so quick to jump to conclusions, General. Bioenergy research on Earth has conclusively proven that certain plant life is able to communicate on a primitive level."

General Augusto glared at the Martian. "So what if it can read ours? All I care about is picking that big brain apart so we can find out what makes them tick. I'm looking for a weakness, Doctor. Something we can exploit to our advantage."

"I'll do whatever you ask of me," Dr. Huffington said. "But it will take time."

General Augusto placed a hand on the Martian and the creature gave a slight shudder. "As docile as this thing has been, we have all the time in the world."

"Peculiar, that," Dr. Huffington said. "It didn't resist at all when it was shackled."

Archard's unease grew. "That doesn't fit what I know of them, General. They're extremely aggressive."

"The lobsters and the crabs, maybe," General Augusto said and gave the yellow carapace a smack. "Their leaders, not so much."

Just then Major Fogarty burst in. "General!"

"You're back already?" General Augusto said. "Where's the drill and the saw?"

"We're getting reports, sir," Major Fogarty said excitedly. "Seismic readings that have been growing in strength."

"Seismic readings from where?" General Augusto said.

Major Fogarty pointed straight down. "From under the colony, sir. And the strongest readings..." He hesitated, his gaze resting on the yellow Martian.

"Spit it out, damn you," General Augusto said.

"The strongest readings, sir," Major Fogarty said, "come from under this very building."

34

"Your idea is insane," Trisna Sahir said. She was holding her daughter Behulah in her left arm and clasping Piotr Zabinski's hand with her other.

"I've been through this horror twice," Dr. Katla Dkany said. "I'll be damned if I'll suffer through another one." Poking her head around the corner, Katla took stock.

Bradbury's Emergency Shelter was a block west of the Admin Center. Intended as a refuge of last resort in the event of a calamity, the shelter contained rations and air tanks and whatever else the colonists might need in a crisis situation. It also kept spare EVA suits.

That last item interested Katla most. To reach the drop ships, they must exit the dome. And they dare not step foot outside without a suit. To do so meant instant death.

Normally, the Shelter was as quiet as a cemetery back on Earth. No one ever had occasion to use it. It wasn't even manned. Or locked.

At the moment, though, several soldiers were standing out in front, talking.

Katla pulled back before they saw her watching them.

"Is something the matter?" Trisna asked.

"They might have posted guards."

"Good. Then we can forget your crazy idea," Trisna said. "Even if by some miracle we gain access to a drop ship, who is going to fly it? I can assure you I'm not. I wouldn't have the first idea how."

"It can't be that hard," Katla said. "The systems are mostly automated."

"Mostly?"

"Besides, I might have misspoke," Katla said. "We don't to steal one."

"Praise Vishnu. You have come to your senses."

"We only need to sneak on board."

Trisna sighed and bowed her head. "Why are you my friend? What did I do to deserve you?"

"I beg your pardon?" Katla said.

"Nothing," Trisna said. "I suppose sneaking on board is wiser than trying to fly one. The punishment for being caught should be much less."

"That's the spirit."

Katla peeked out again and was delighted to see that the troopers had gone off down the street. Plucking at Trisna's sleeve, she said, "Quick. Before anyone else comes by."

Entry was gained by tapping a code into an access panel, and the code was plainly stamped for anyone to use. Katla punched in the mix of numbers and letters, the panel light turned green, and the door opened with a slight hiss. She pulled Trisna in after her as the overhead lights automatically came on.

"We're in!"

"Lucky us," Trisna said.

The EVA suits were on racks near the front. Beyond were scores of shelves piled high with supplies.

Anxiously, Katla inspected the suits. They were older models, the kind colonists used in the early days. Bulky, but serviceable. She was afraid there wouldn't be any small enough for the children but on the last rack were several that would fit Behulah and Piotr.

"We're in luck."

"If you want to think so, fine."

Katla turned. "We have to work together, Trisna, or we'll never make it off-planet. And unless we do, we're as good as dead."

"You don't know that."

Katla gestured at Behulah and Piotr. "It's not just us we have to consider."

"I know," Trisna said, and gave her daughter a tender kiss on the cheek. "They are why I am here. Were it just me, I would let you go your merry way and come visit you in prison."

"Funny lady."

"I didn't mean it to be."

It took much longer than Katla liked to shrug and tug into the EVA suits and to figure out the control pads on the sleeves. Then each air tank had to be checked to verify it was full.

Finally, they were ready.

"We'll carry our helmets," she said. "It might look suspicious if we put them on before we reach the airlock."

"How do you know they will even let us through?" Trisna said.

"I'll say 'pretty please.'"

"I must say, it is a shock to have known you so long and only now realize you need counseling." Trisna grinned as she said it.

Katla peered out the window to be sure the coast was clear. "Stay close. And whatever happens, don't become separated." She held out her hand to Piotr.

"Hold tight to me," Trisna said to Behulah. "And if I set you down and tell you to run, do so."

"Yes, mother."

Katla went out first, looked both ways, and motioned. Smiling, she adopted a casual air, strolling along as if she didn't have a care in the world.

Trying hard to imitate her, Trisna said, "How can you be so calm? My brain is screaming at me to forget this madness and go have some tea."

Passers-by paid no particular attention. EVA suits were common, after all.

Katla came to an intersection and turned right onto Carter Street.

"Where are you going?" Trisna said. "I thought you were heading for the airlock."

"The main airlock will have soldiers going in and out," Katla figured. "We're better off using the smaller lock on the south side."

"You know best," Trisna said in a tone that hinted she had her doubts.

"I hope we get there before all hell breaks loose."

"Ever the optimist," Trisna said dryly, and suddenly stopped. "Wait. Do you feel that?"

The ground under them was shaking. The tremors weren't strong enough to cause them to lose their balance but the effect was unnerving.

"Katla?" Piotr said fearfully.

"An earthquake, do you think?" Trisna said.

Before Katla could answer, the ground shook even harder, and from the bowels of Mars there issued a loud rumble.

35

There were days when Private Everett missed the hills of his native Kentucky so much it hurt. Days when he wondered what in the world he was thinking when he volunteered for duty on Mars. Sure, he earned three times his pay grade. But it hadn't been just about the money.

He'd always liked to explore. When he was a boy, the Kentucky backwoods had been an unknown realm rife with adventure. He'd always hankered to know what lay over that next ridge, over that next hill.

He supposed it was only natural that when he grew up, he hankered to see what lay on the next planet.

Still, at moments like this, he could kick himself for being so naïve. Twice now, through sheer, dumb luck, he had managed to survive the destruction of a colony. But no one's luck held forever. The third time might be the end of his string.

As Captain Ferris studied the screen graph of the seismic activity their sensors were picking up, Everett gazed longingly at the golden domes they were protecting. He wondered where his friends were; Private Pasco, Dr. Dkany, that Hindu gal, and Captain Rahn.

"Picking up motion, Captain!" the tech trooper announced.

"Underground?" Captain Ferris said.

"No," the trooper responded, and pointed toward the stark Martian terrain beyond. "Out there, ma'am."

Without being told to, Everett scrambled up the trench and poked his head over the rim.

Private Keller joined him. "Do you see what I see?"

Private Everett frowned. How could he miss it? A gigantic cloud of dust was rising all along the far horizon.

"A dust storm, you think?" Private Keller said.

Everett pondered. Dust storms weren't uncommon. Instead of wind, it was the sun that caused them. The atmosphere was so thin, that when the sun warmed it, it caused the air to move, whisking up a lot of fine dust in the process. But in this case, he said, "No."

"Why not?"

"Too much, too fast, over too wide an area," was Everett's assessment.

"Dust storms can be that big. Bigger even," Keller said. "Remember the global ones?"

"Yeah," Everett said. The last superstorm, as they were called, had been three years ago. "This feels different."

"You can feel dust?" Keller teased.

Everett realized Captain Ferris was beside them and was impressed. He hadn't heard her come up.

"I think Private Everett is right."

Sergeant Kline materialized at her elbow. "So the dust is rising in a giant circle with us in the middle? You know what that makes us?"

"What?" Private Keller said.

"The bullseye."

Everett swore. "The critters have skunked us and made our drop ships next to useless."

"Oh, hell," Captain Ferris said.

"Ma'am?" Private Keller said.

"He's right again," Captain Ferris said. "All that dust would wreak havoc with the drop ship engines. They won't be able to provide air support."

"It will also mess up our sensors," Everett said. "Bigtime."

"Hell, hell, hell," Captain Ferris said.

"Wait a minute," Private Keller said. "Are you two saying that the Martians are doing it on purpose?"

"That would be my guess," Everett said.

"No need to panic," Captain Ferris said. "We have enough firepower to mow them down right and left."

"You really think so, ma'am?" Private Keller said.

"They can't get anywhere close," Captain Ferris predicted. "We've overlapped the field of fire of our gun emplacements so that each supports the others to either side. It would take a zillion Martians to break through."

In the short time they were talking, the cloud had grown twice as large.

"More motion, Captain!" the tech specialist hollered.

"Out there?" Ferris said, nodding.

"No, ma'am. Under our feet."

"What?" Captain Ferris jumped down to the bottom of the trench and moved to the tech's station.

Everett nudged Keller and followed.

The sensor screen displayed a legion of huge shapes deep underground. Shapes that were crisscrossing back and forth in a definite pattern. The seismic indicators were going crazy.

"What the hell are those things?" Captain Ferris said. "There must be hundreds of them."

An icy chill swept through Everett. "Those are Martian borers, sir. The creatures that make their tunnels."

"And they're digging away at the dirt under us?" Captain Ferris said in alarm. "Do you know what that means?"

The ground began to rumble and shake.

36

Captain Archard Rahn's worst fear was coming to pass. The Martians were attacking the third colony. The floor and walls had begun to shake and he was certain it would only grow worse. "General, we have to get out of here."

"Nonsense," General Augusto said.

The entire cell gave a lurch and Archard nearly lost his balance. It was if the floor were falling out from under them. A second tremor made him realize it wasn't the floor; it was the entire building.

"What's going on?" General Augusto demanded. "Speak to me, Fogarty."

The major was listening to his commlink and had paled. "It's the Martians, sir."

"What about them, damn it?"

"They appear to be digging away at the dirt under us."

A third, more powerful jolt, sent Archard to one knee. His EVA suit absorbed most of the force, but the pain still made him wince. Others weren't so fortunate. A trooper pitched face-first against a wall and left a bloody smear. A scientist fell onto the monitoring console, his hand gave a loud crack, and he cried out.

"It's happening all over Bradbury," Major Fogarty said. "The Martians are undermining the entire colony."

For the first time since Archard met him, General Constantine Augusto was too shocked to speak. With a visible effort, he gathered himself and activated his own commlink. "This is General Augusto to all units and personnel. We're under assault from below. Troopers not assigned to specific posts will report to U.N.I.C. HQ, ASAP. All others, defend and protect."

Major Fogarty made bold to grab the general's forearm. "We should leave, sir, as Captain Rahn suggested. Immediately."

"I'm not going anywhere without my prisoner," Augusto said.

The creature, Archard noticed, had turned its eye stalks toward the floor. The implication was like a blow to his gut. "General!" he shouted to be heard above the rumbling. "You have to head topside! The Martians are coming after you, personally!"

"Nonsense, Captain," General Augusto said. "They don't know who or where I am."

"Yes, they do," Archard said, gesturing at the yellow Martian. "Don't you see? It can communicate with the rest of its kind."

"We haven't established that they are indeed telepathic," General Augusto said skeptically.

"Accept that they are," Archard urged. "And leave. Please. Before it's too late."

The building shook to the most violent quake yet---and the floor began to slide out from under them. Slowly but steadily it was sinking into the ground.

Major Fogarty turned to the BioMarines. "Get the general out of here! Now!"

Moving was difficult. Archard started toward the door but it was like walking on the deck of a pitching boat.

The BioMarines, though, didn't seem to be affected. They sprang to either side of the general and seized him by the arms.

"What in God's name do you think you're doing?" Augusto bellowed. "Release me this instant!"

The tall form of KLL-1 filled the doorway. "No! Bring the general. We must keep him alive at all costs!"

"Let go of me, damn you!" Augusto raged. "This is rank insubordination!"

Archard reached the door and gripped the frame for support. He made it out, the floor tilting more with every step. When he reached the elevator, the emergency lights were flashing. Rather than risk being trapped inside on the way up, he moved to the stairwell and shouldered the door open.

"Hold that for us, if you please," KLL-1 said.

Archard did, and the pair of BioMarines holding onto General Augusto filed past, the general continuing to rage.

More BioMarines and troopers went through. Back in the interrogation room, someone shouted something. Screams and autofire erupted.

Archard was about to go back in to help when a soldier ran out into the hall, yelling, "Go! Go! Martians are pouring in! They've rescued their leader!"

His pulse racing, Archard fled up the stairs. If the same thing was happening all over Bradbury, this was a disaster in the making. The Martians were employing a whole new tactic, to devastating effect. Keying his private channel, he called, "Katla? Katla? Are you there? Can you hear me?

There was no reply.

Archard shuddered to think what she must be going through up above. He prayed she stayed alive long enough for him to find her.

Provided he stayed alive, himself.

37

At first, Dr. Katla Dkany thought it was an earthquake. Mars experienced fewer than Earth, in large part because Mars had fewer tectonic plates. As the ground under them shook and shimmied, she flung out both arms to keep her balance and heard a great rending rasp, as if two slabs of stone were being rubbed together.

Glancing up, Katla beheld an astounding sight. The building across the street was sinking. The entire bottom floor was already below ground level, and from inside came screams and wails.

"What's happening?" Trisna Sahir cried, clutching Behulah.

Katla saw a building down the block begin to sink. A plume of dust signaled a third was about to do the same.

"Katla?" Piotr said.

From all quarters rose more horrendous rending and rasping sounds, as well as the crash of shattering glass.

"What is happening?" Trisna again cried. "What is this madness?"

"It must be the Martians," Katla said.

As if to prove her right, out of a broken window in a building across the street scuttled a reddish-pink crab, its grippers waving.

A man wasn't three meters from it, frozen in stunned disbelief. He screamed as the creature launched itself at his chest.

"Not again!" Trisna cried.

Firming her grip on Piotr, Katla headed down the street. "Run! Or we'll be next!"

The man's shrieks were hideous. He was on his back, and not one but two Martians were on top of him. One held him down while the other used its grippers to clamp hold of either side of his head. With a brutal wrench, the Martian tore it from his body.

Behulah commenced bawling.

Katla ran as fast as her bulky EVA suit permitted. Thinking of it reminded her of another danger. Suddenly stopping, she shouted, "Our helmets! Put them on!"

Trisna nodded. She understood the consequences should Dome One be breached.

They assisted Piotr and Behulah in putting theirs on as bedlam reigned around them. Then on they ran, Katla more intent than ever on reaching the secondary airlock. A drop ship was their only hope. Unless they could get off-planet, it would be Wellsville and New Meridian all over again.

Her earphones crackled, and she thought she heard her name. "Archard?" she said, boosting the gain. "Is that you?"

All she heard was the sizzle of static.

Katla kept going.

More and more buildings were being swallowed by the Martian earth. Some had tilted. Some were buckling. Smaller residential modules were gobbled whole. The din of breakage and ruin was catastrophic, punctuated by screeches and sobs and curses. Terrified colonists rushed helter-skelter. Troopers were trying to help as best as they were able.

Katla shut everything from her mind except reaching the airlock. She rounded a corner and collided with a woman coming the other way. If not for Trisna catching hold of her, she would have been bowled over.

Three blocks away stood the airlock. It might as well be on one of the Martian moons. The street was jammed with people. A tall building, partially sunk, was in danger of falling across it. And there were Martians, many of them, coming out of windows and doors and through the very walls. Firefights broke out, the troopers rallying to resist the invaders.

Crouching with her arms protectively over Behulah, Trisna shouted, "We need to find cover! Somewhere safe!"

"Keep up with me!" Katla was certain that to stop was a death warrant. On an impulse, she darted into an alley and ran along it to the next street. Her hope was that there would be fewer people but it wasn't to be.

The buildings in their vicinity were still standing although a few were shaking. Katla skirted recessed steps that led down into a shadowed doorway from which a pair of legs in uniform jutted. Under the legs, a pool of blood had formed.

Katla abruptly stopped. Halfway down the steps lay an ICW. Archard had shown her how to use them. Letting go of Piotr, she darted down, snatched it up, and checked the magazine. It was full. The trooper had been slain before he could get off a shot. She set the weapon to three-round bursts instead of full auto, and went back up to the others.

A man ran past, shrieking at the top of his lungs. "Run! Run! The monsters are everywhere!"

A woman missing an arm and pumping blood staggered toward them from the other side of the street but collapsed.

"What are we waiting for?" Trisna said.

"Take Piotr," Katla said. She needed both hands free to shoot.

Out of an office building stumbled a man with a Martian on his back, its grippers tearing at his flesh like cleavers.

Katla shot it, aiming at the top of its carapace as Archard had instructed her. The creature fell and thrashed and was still. Its victim went another couple of strides and sprawled flat.

They reached the end of the street. Only one block separated them from the airlock, and there were less people.

Katla glanced out the dome toward the hanger and the airstrip, and her resolve faltered. Almost the entire sky was filled with a great roiling cloud of dust that rose hundreds of meters into the air---and was about to engulf the drop ships.

38

Like an immense living thing composed of swirling nanoparticles, the dust cloud swept toward Bradbury's three golden domes. Warnings were flashed all along the perimeter. Be ready for anything.

Captain Ferris had gone to the maser emplacement at the east end of the trench, taking Sergeant Kline with her.

Leaving Everett and Private Keller to contemplate the rapidly approaching dust storm.

Everett wanted no part of it. In his opinion, the general had made a dire blunder. They were more vulnerable outside the domes, at the mercy of not only the Martians but basic atmospherics. A single puncture of their EVA suits was all it would take. A hole sufficiently large that the suit's self-repair system was unable to seal, and decompression would do them in.

"What do you think, Kentucky?" Private Keller asked, using her external helmet mic rather than her commlink.

"Biggest FUBAR ever," Everett said.

"What can we do?"

"We can't desert our posts," Everett said.

"If only."

They looked at one another and Everett said, "We stick as long as we can. Then we try for an airlock."

"Agreed," Keller said. "Wish we were inside now." She looked at the dome behind them and stiffened. "What the hell? What's going on in there?"

Everett wasn't sure. The buildings were shaking. Incredibly, some appeared to be shrinking. He blinked, seeking to make sense of it.

"They're sinking!" Keller cried.

"Dear Lord," Everett breathed.

Entire structures were slowly sliding into the ground, like so many plants being pulled under by gophers.

"I'm seeing it and I don't believe it," Keller said.

Everett believed it. The Martians were devious as could be. Instead of burrowing up out of the ground to attack the colonists in the streets and in their homes, as they had done at the other colonies, their huge borers were digging away the entire foundation, bedrock and all, to bring the humans down to them. "I'll be switched."

"You'll be what?"

"Nothing," Everett said and faced the dust cloud. From one improbable to another. The cloud's leading edge wasn't more than a hundred meters out and had stopped. It was so high, it blotted out most of the sunlight. Their trench, and the gun emplacements, were plunged in shadow.

"Can this get any worse?" Keller said.

At the base of the cloud, in the depths of the dust, vague figures moved.

"Those Martians devils," Everett said. "They learned their lesson at New Meridian and Wellsville. Instead of going head-to-head, they're being sneaky."

A buzzing sound drew their attention to a U.N.I.C. drone flying along the trench toward them. A surveillance model, it was used to spy on enemy positions.

"A drone can't see much in all that dust," Private Keller said.

Apparently, whoever was using it thought differently. Rising to half the height of the cloud, the drone flew directly into it. For a few second, its silhouette was visible, then it was gone.

"If you ask me," Keller said, "a waste of a good drone."

No sooner were the words out of her mouth then the drone reappeared. Sputtering and spitting sparks, it wobbled erratically while spiraling lower and lower until finally it crashed a stone's throw away.

Captain Ferris ran up, talking into her commlink. "No, sir. I just saw it with my own eyes. I don't know what took it out but it wasn't able to penetrate very far. Yes, sir. Understood. We will await your command." She climbed next to them and hunkered. "That was the colonel. We can expect to engage any moment now."

"Engage what, sir?" Private Keller said, indicating the cloud. "We can't see to shoot."

"We're pouring everything we have into it," Captain Ferris said. "If that's not enough…"

Private Everett flicked a hand at the dome. "How bad is it in there?"

"Let the troopers inside deal with inside," Captain Ferris said. "You worry about out here." She tilted her head as if listening to a communication, then straightened and barked on her detachment's frequency, "All personnel! Open fire! I repeat! All guns, all troopers, lay into them!"

Private Everett propped his elbow on the rim, pointed his ICW at the cloud, and cut loose. All along the line, troopers were doing the same. The masers and lasers and ion cannon opened up, unleashing a barrage that would reduce terrestrial foes to atoms. Beams of light crisscrossed the cloud like a light show, only these were deadly. Shells burst and explosions thundered.

"Are we killing anything?" Private Keller yelled.

They had to be, Everett thought. Nothing could withstand such an onslaught. But was it enough to drive their attackers back?

No.

Martians spilled out of the dust in a torrent. Red Martians, blue Martians, the black flyers, and others. In a wave of carapaces and grippers and eye stalks, they swept toward the Earthers like the tide toward a beach.

The Martians had timed their attack perfectly. For even as they rushed toward the trenches and the gun emplacements, the dust cloud descended to cover everyone and everything.

Everett found himself fighting in a pea-soup. Or, rather, a dust-soup, that limited his vision and the effectiveness of his sensors. Exactly as the Martians intended. He let fly with a frag grenade and then an incendiary.

The masers were thrumming, the lasers flashing, the ion cannons adding their thunder.

The Martians died in droves but his motion sensors told Everett they were still coming.

As if that wasn't enough, the ground under them suddenly began to buckle.

39

The BioMarines led the escape to the surface. KLL-12 and KLL-13, with four others, were ordered to take point by KLL-1 and were ahead of the rest, climbing the stairs in long bounds.

The chatter on KLL-12's commlink told him that General Augusto and his top aides were being protected by KLL-1 and ten more BioMarines, while the remaining seven hybrids were bringing up the rear with Captain Archard Rahn and some humans.

"Having fun yet?" KLL-13 said with her invariable laugh.

KLL-12 failed to appreciate her humor. "The colony is under assault but you find it humorous?"

"Life is humorous," she said. "You take it all way too seriously."

The building gave yet another violent shake, nearly throwing them off balance. The walls, KLL-12 noticed, were tilting at an ever-steeper angle. Thankfully, with their enhanced abilities, they could cling with their toes to any surface short of oil-coated glass.

KLL-12's commlink crackled anew.

"Point team," KLL-1 said. "Don't get too far ahead. The general and his staff can't go very fast."

KLL-12 reached the next landing and read the digital display. He keyed his mic. "KLL-1. We're at Level Five. How far back at you?"

"We've just passed eight," KLL-1 replied.

Over by the rail, KLL-17 said to KLL-12, "We should wait for them to catch up."

"I agree," KLL-13 said.

From above and around them came crackling noises and intermittent rumbling. A thin crack appeared in a wall.

"I hope this place doesn't collapse on us," KLL-15 remarked.

"If you got to go, you got to go," KLL-13 said.

"What?" KLL-15 said.

"Ignore her," KLL-12 said. "She's insane."

"Hold on a second," KLL-13 said, bending her head toward the wall with the crack. "Do you hear that?"

KLL-12 did. A muted grinding, growing louder. It reminded him of the sound a drill made, only lower in pitch.

"Be ready for anything," KLL-14 said.

"That's my middle name," KLL-13 said.

The grinding rose to a piercing crescendo. The next moment, the center of the wall dissolved into shards and pieces. A cloud of dust spewed out, followed by the serrated carapace of a giant Martian borer. The whirling crown that comprised its drill thrust at the landing like the tip of a spear.

Springing back, KLL-12 prepared to leap over the rail. But he didn't have to. The borer came to a stop an arm's-length away. Its eyes rose on long stalks out of hidden recesses and swiveled about as if it were trying to get its bearings. Suddenly, it saw them, and just-like-that, its eye stalks retracted and it slid back into the hole it had made.

"Get ready," KLL-12 warned. "You know what's coming next."

"Martians," KLL-13 said.

The creatures poured out of the hole. Eye stalks waving, their grippers spread, they were on the BioMarines in a twinkling.

"We're under attack!" KLL-12 reported on his commlink and sprang to meet them. He bashed. He smashed. He tore. He rent. Constantly in motion, turning this way and that, he battled furiously. He lost track of how many creatures he killed, and how many wounds they inflicted. He was aware that his healing ability was being taxed to its utmost but he couldn't worry about that right now. He must fight, fight, fight.

KLL-12 was also aware that his fellow hybrids were battling just as furiously but he dared not risk a glance to see how they were faring.

A cry told him one of the others had gone down. A shout in his commlink from KLL-13 told him who.

"KLL-14! They got her!"

"Don't give up!" KLL-12 roared. He expected KLL-1 to send others to help them but his hope was dashed when his commlink blared yet again.

"KLL-1 is down! KLL-1 is down! This is KLL-3! We are under attack too! We need..."

Her transmission ended.

Faintly, KLL-12 heard another report, from lower down.

"........KLL-24............under heavy................repeat......
...request assistance...request..."

His transmission faded away.

"They're hitting all of us at once!" KLL-13 hollered. "What do we do?"

To KLL-12, it was obvious. They must think of their own lives before all else. But he couldn't break his programming. He was compelled to follow orders, and their orders were to get General Augusto to the surface. Evading a lunging Martian, he keyed his mic again. "General Augusto? Are you there? Respond, please!"

His earphones filled with static.

"General Augusto! Confirm that you are still alive!" KLL-12 requested.

More crackling ensued.

"KLL-1? KLL-3? Anyone at all?" KLL-12 said.

Amid a flurry of motion, a headless body tumbled through the air and landed almost at KLL-12's feet.

"KLL-16!" KLL-13 cried. "They tore his head off!"

Ducking and dodging grippers that lanced at his neck and chest, KLL-12 came to a decision. Out in the open, he and the other BioMarines stood half a chance.

But down here, in the cramped confines of the stairs, with more Martians streaming in every second, it was hopeless. The outcome was inevitable.

"BioMarines!" KLL-12 shouted. "On me! General Augusto has been slain! Make for the surface or we are as good as dead!"

No one disputed him. Not even KLL-13, who was caked with Martian blood and who, for once, had lost her mischievous grin.

Exerting himself to his utmost, KLL-12 sought to break free of the press of crustoids and gain the next landing. He saw that only four of them were left; himself, KLL-13, KLL-15, and KLL-17. The latter had sustained a severe wound that caused him to limp.

A red Martian leaped at KLL-12, its grippers snapping. Sidestepping, KLL-12 seized it by two of its legs and swung the creature in an arc, using it to batter other Martians aside. He split a carapace, sheared off eye stalks, smashed a scuttling menace. Then, to his relief, he was momentarily in the clear.

KLL-13 and KLL-15 had emulated him and came up shoulder-to-shoulder.

KLL-17, still limping, tried to spring above a closing circle of Martians. His leg must have given way because he pitched into his foes instead. Like piranha tearing at a horse, the Martians tore KLL-17 to bits, one of them claiming his head.

"Run!" KLL-12 shouted. He threw the creature he was carrying to forestall a rush. It bought them the seconds they needed to whirl and flee, taking the steps five at a time.

"Still having fun?" KLL-12 snapped at KLL-13 as they reached the next landing.

Her face smeared with gore, she smiled and said, "Bite me."

For some reason, KLL-12 laughed.

40

General Constantine Augusto was fit to be tied. Despite his meticulous planning, everything was falling apart.

The worst aspect was having his own brilliance used against him. He was certain that capturing a Martian leader was crucial to ultimate victory. The fact that their two species couldn't communicate was of piddling concern. He'd had every confidence his science people and the psych department could crack the Martian open like a hammer cracking a nut and have the thing spilling its secrets in no time.

He'd never imagined the creatures would use his master stroke against him. That his prisoner could become the focal point---by somehow drawing the other Martians to it---for an attack on U.N.I.C. headquarters.

And now here he was, on the run, fleeing up the stairs with his subordinates and about half the BioMarines.

Above them, bedlam had broken out. His commlink was a jumble of panicked cries and appeals for help.

Major Fogarty, at his elbow, said urgently, "General, I've just received a report that the Martians have engaged our perimeter defenses."

"Damn it to hell," General Augusto fumed. "I need to get up there. I can't direct a war from this stairwell."

"That's not all," Major Fogarty said. "It isn't just HQ that's being undermined. The Martians are digging under the entire colony. Buildings all over are sliding into the ground."

As if to accent that point, HQ lurched and tilted, nearly pitching General Augusto to his knees. Fortunately, a large reptilian hand swooped down and steadied him.

"Sir!" KLL-1 said. "My point squad and rear guard are under attack."

"The BioMarines can more than hold their own," General Augusto said. "We keep going."

"I recommend we expedite your extraction," KLL-1 said. "Let me and some of the others carry you up."

"Carry me?" Augusto said.

"We can go a lot faster that way," KLL-1 said.

"Like a damn baby?"

"Please. Your safety is paramount."

General Augusto would burn in hell before he would let his men see him being carried. "I can manage on my own, thank you very much."

"But sir…" KLL-1 began and got no further.

The walls on either side exploded as borer Martians broke through. One instant they were there, the next they had withdrawn, leaving gaping holes that were filled by scuttling torrents of the small red crabs.

"Protect the general!" KLL-1 bellowed, and the BioMarines and the troopers went into action, the hybrids forming a living barrier between the Martians and Augusto, the soldiers opening up with their ICW's.

A mad melee ensued, savage combat with no quarter given.

General Augusto tried to draw his sidearm, a Tactical LASR, but was jostled by his protectors and nearly lost his grip. Using both hands, he raised it and pressed the stud that engaged the nanocircuitry. The LASR was so expensive to manufacture that they were only issued to officers at the highest echelons. They were worth every penny. As the acronym implied, they were miniature lasers, able to slice through organic and inorganic matter like a hot knife through butter.

Augusto centered his LASR's sights on the Martians pouring from the left-side hole and fired. A vivid red beam literally cut creatures in two. Careful not to hit the BioMarines and troopers struggling all around him, he felled over twenty Martians, slowing their attack. Smiling grimly, he switched to the other entry point and slew a slew of crustoids.

Augusto was thrilled to his core to be in combat again. It had been ages since he last risked his own hide like this. These days, he fought from behind the scenes, the puppet master who sent other men and women to live or die for the greater good of all humanity.

A falling body knocked him sideways and brought him out of himself. Startled, he looked down, and his breath caught in his throat.

KLL-1 lay at his feet, a score of wounds in various stages of healing that would never occur because half of KLL-1's face was missing. His remaining eye seemed to focus on Augusto, then glazed over.

General Augusto glanced up. Only now did he realize that more than half the BioMarines were down and but a few troopers were left. He didn't see Major Fogarty. He turned to run, and a red Martian sprang. In reflex, he cored it with his LASR.

"General!" one of the remaining troopers hollered.

General Augusto swung toward him in time to see the man's head ripped from his body.

Martians continued to stream from the holes in twin rivers of carapaces.

General Augusto fired, backpedaled, fired again. He spun and fired. He dodged and fired.

The last trooper died screamed.

Only a couple of BioMarines were alive and they were crawling with Martians.

Dazed at how swiftly they had been beaten, Augusto stumbled over bodies to the rail. He would not be taken alive. He would take a header and die as a soldier should. Firing right and left, he gripped the rail and prepared to hurtle to his doom. But even as he raised his leg, his other leg was seized by a Martian gripper. Twisting, he pointed his LASR but another creature clamped onto his wrist and pushed his arm up. He fired anyway, and a third Martian wrenched the LASR from his grasp.

In the blink of an eye, General Augusto's remaining arm and leg were clamped tight. With disheartening swiftness, four of the things bore him over the piles of dead and into the dark maw of a jagged hole.

41

Captain Archard Rahn and the rest of the flankers reached the next landing. *So far, so good*, he thought. But he was only kidding himself. He and those with him---seven BioMarines and five troopers---weren't enough to stem a swarm. He only hoped the Martians were content with rescuing their leader.

More rumbling from below resulted in another sharp shift in the stairs. Archard was able to keep his balance, barely.

"I hate this," a trooper with the name Cavanaugh on his uniform complained. "I feel so helpless."

"Buck up, Corporal," Archard said by way of encouragement he didn't feel. "Once we're topside, we'll be all right."

"If we get there," Corporal Cavanaugh said dispiritedly.

Archard kept an eye on the stairs behind them. The Martian's hadn't appeared yet but they were bound to come pouring out of the interrogation room any moment.

One of the BioMarines came to his side, a female. "Captain," she said. "I'm KLL-18."

His attention still on the stairs, Archard responded, "Pleased to meet you."

"I'm in constant contact with KLL-1," she informed him. "He has the general, and they are about two levels above us."

"Good," Archard said. But he was thinking that the general should be moving faster.

Bending, KLL-18 said so only he would hear, "You are the ranking officer in this group. You should be aware of the sounds we are hearing."

"Sounds?" Archard said.

KLL-18 nodded. "Our hearing is more acute than yours." She nodded at the walls. "We are picking up noises. They are not clear but something is happening on the other side."

"What can it be but Martians?"

"I suggest we hurry and catch up to General Augusto. There is strength in numbers, as you humans like to say. KLL-1 agrees. He told me to talk to you. He is worried for the general's safety."

"Pick up the pace, then," Archard said, and managed a lopsided smile. "Us humans will do our best to keep up."

KLL-18 gestured, and the BioMarines increased their speed. So did Archard and the other troopers.

Archard noticed that KLL-18 and the other hybrids had formed a square around him and his men. The BioMarines weren't being obvious about it but they clearly intended to protect the soldiers.

"Decent of you," Archard told her.

"Sorry?" she said.

Archard swept an arm at her and her fellows.

"We are conditioned to put human welfare before our own," KLL-18 said. "But I would do it anyway."

"Oh?" Archard said. The small talk was helping to take his mind off Katla.

"We are U.N.I.C.," KLL-18 said. "We always have each other's backs, yes?"

"Booyah," Archard said.

"Exactly so," she said, grinning.

They came to another landing. The two BioMarines in the lead had stopped and were standing close to a wall, their ears practically touching it.

"What do you hear?" KLL-18 said.

One of them opened his mouth to answer but whatever he said was drowned out by the grinding din of a giant borer exploding through the wall above him. Debris and dust rained down, obscuring the living drill for the seconds the creature took to withdrawn from the huge hole it had made.

Through the opening streamed Martians.

The two BioMarines below the hole were buried under an avalanche of crustoids.

"Close up! Close up!" Archard bellowed, and opened fire. In the confines of the stairwell, they stood a better chance back-to-back. The troopers near him complied, adding their firepower to his.

KLL-18 and the remaining BioMarines formed a line in-between and met the Martians rush with a ferocity that had to be seen to be believed. They smashed, they crushed, they tore limbs.

The initial charge faltered but it was only temporary. A river of Martians continued to flow through the hole, more than enough to replace those that had fallen. KLL-18 and her test-tube kindred fell back a few steps but then held their ground, refusing to give another centimeter.

The combat became a blur of slaughter and gore.

Archard and the troopers did what they could to help, downing Martians when clear shots presented themselves.

Archard was so intent on doing what he could for the hybrids that he didn't realize the mistake he was making in not watching his own back until Corporal Cavanaugh gave a piercing yell.

"Behind us! Good God, they're behind us, too!"

Martians were scrambling up the stairs. There were so many, they covered not only the steps but the rails and the walls.

"Frags!" Archard commanded and triggered a grenade at optimum range.

The blasts were near-deafening, even with Archard's helmet baffles. The explosions shook the stairwell and left a pulped heap of mangled Martians.

A new tide of creatures flowed over the slain. Forelimbs spread, grippers splayed, they sought to close with the human invaders of their planet.

"Frags again!" Archard roared. "On my mark." He aimed his ICW. "Now!"

Five weapons chuffed in unison, lobbing five grenades that detonated simultaneously. Martians were pulverized.

Archard heard a cry of agony behind him but he didn't dare look to see how the BioMarines were doing. Raising his ICW, he roared, "Incendiaries!"

Sheets of flame engulfed the creatures, incinerating some and turning others into wildly careening fireballs. The heat was blistering.

This time, the Martians were slower to recover.

Archard risked a glance over his shoulder.

Only four of the seven BioMarines were still alive. KLL-18 was one of them, and she and her companions were slaying with brutal efficiency.

"Here they come again!" Corporal Cavanaugh hollered.

The flames were dwindling and the Martians had regrouped.

"Autofire!" Archard shouted.

A withering hailstorm met the foremost Martians, turning their carapaces into the crustacean equivalent of Swiss cheese. Scores fell, but scores more filled the gaps.

"Back up!" Archard yelled to gain them room but they had nowhere to go. The BioMarines were at their backs.

"Give them hell!" Archard shouted, and did so, shooting and shooting, constantly shifting as targets presented themselves. Everything became a whirl of movement and death. He was jostled. Bumped. Nearly bowled over. He dropped a crab lunging at his legs, shot another in midair. He heard Corporal Cavanaugh yell and a scream of mortal terror. Martians were all over. A BioMarine battled on his left and a trooper fought on his right and the dying and dead were in piles. He fired yet again. A blow to his hip staggered him. He felt a gripper on his arm and then a tremendous jolt to his head and he pitched forward onto dead Martians. Something heavy crashed onto his back and then the jumble of sensations were erased by a black emptiness and there was nothing, nothing at all.

42

To call it bedlam did not do it justice.

As the massive cloud descended, so did a preternatural twilight. From out of the murk rose screams and curses and gurgling rattles that ended in death wails.

The United Nations Interplanetary Command had planned for every contingency. Or so they thought. Their experts never imagined that the denizens of the Red Planet would use *dust* as a weapon. Nor did it occur to the big brains that instead of being content with burrowing up into a colony through random tunnels, the Martians might elect to undermine a colony's entire foundation by excavating the very earth out from under them.

All this went through Private Everett's mind as the ground under him rumbled and shook and a phalanx of crustaceans scrabbled over the uneven terrain toward the trench he was defending. The dust was so thick that he could barely make them out.

Everett poured autofire into the horde. Beside him, Private Keller did the same. Somewhere on his right side, Captain Ferris was firing, and on the other Sergeant Kline was bellowing something or other.

Everett's skin crawled at the prospect of being overrun. An inevitable outcome, given their numbers and the fact that their masers, lasers and ion cannons were being effectively neutralized by the dust. Since the Martians didn't register on infrared, targeting had to be done using motion sensors, and the motion sensors were going haywire trying to distinguish between the particles of swirling dust and discreet targets.

The masers and lasers and cannons were still firing but not as effectively, as the chatter on Everett's commlink made clear.

His magazine went empty and Everett ejected it and slapped in a new one. He looked up just as a red Martian sprang out of the dust at his face. He recoiled, bracing for the worst, and in that split-second, a burst of autofire cut it down.

Sergeant Kline materialized. "Where's the captain?" he yelled. "I can't raise her."

Everett pointed. "Over yonder. I lost track of her in all this dust."

"You and Keller are on me," Sergeant Kline said, and dashed past them.

"You heard the man, Kentucky," Keller said, firing as she backpedaled.

Staying at her side, Everett sprayed lead. Whether he scored or not he couldn't say.

Keller slapped in a new magazine of her own. "We are off-the-scale screwed."

"Tell me about it," Everett said, boosting the gain on his helmet mic to its limit. He heard none of the telltale scritching that would warn him the Martins were close, although up and down the line a battle royal continued to rage.

Private Keller twisted around. "I can't even see the colony. It's got to be bad there, too, don't you think?"

"The last we saw, buildings were sliding into the ground," Everett said. "So yeah."

The trench gave a violent heave as if it were alive and a crack appeared practically under their feet.

"They must be digging underneath us!" Keller cried.

Everett jumped over the crack and went faster. It was discouraging how the Martians had outwitted them, completely and thoroughly. But he refused to give up. "All that matters is we're alive."

"Knock on wood," Keller said.

The firing along their trench had lessened. Behind them, an ion cannon was giving the Martians as much hell as it could by firing at random into the dust cloud.

In front of them, figures moved, and Keller shouted, "Look out!"

"Don't shoot!" Everett said, pushing her arm aside.

It was Sergeant Kline and Captain Ferris, the noncom supporting the officer. The captain's face was contorted in pain and her right arm hung limp. Additionally, there was a rip in the pant leg of her EVA suit. Kline motioned for them to hunker and carefully lowered Ferris to a knee.

"How bad, ma'am?" Everett said, afraid decompression would claim her life any instant.

"My suit is sealing," Captain Ferris said through clenched teeth. "But I think my arm is broken. Maybe a couple of ribs, too. One of those big blue Martians got me down before I could kill it."

Sergeant Kline said, "The word is, the colony is about to fall. No one can raise the general, and an evacuation has been ordered."

"By who?" Private Keller said.

"Does it matter?" Sergeant Kline replied. "We're getting out of here. That is, if the captain has no objections."

Ferris bit her lower lip and shook her head. "I sure as blazes don't. We need to reach the drop ships, Sergeant. They're our only hope."

"We stay close together," Sergeant Kline said to Everett and Keller. "Watch each other's backs."

"Goes without saying," Private Keller said.

"I'm saying it anyway," Sergeant Kline said, and with Captain Ferris propped against him, started off.

Private Everett swallowed. His mouth was so dry, it hurt to try. "Let's hope the drop ships wait for us."

"I'm trying to raise them," Sergeant Kline said.

"I'm telling you right now," Private Keller said. "If I make it off this damn planet, I'm never coming back."

Everett was about to say he felt the same but the noncom told them to hush up, and listen.

A faint sound filled Everett's earphones. At first, he couldn't place it. Then the truth dawned. Something was coming toward the trench, sliding on the ground like a snake might.

Or a Martian.

43

Dr. Katla Dkany wanted to scream her frustration to the heavens. Twice, she had barely survived the fall of a colony. Now she was going through the same horrific disaster again. The Martians had Bradbury surrounded. Buildings were sliding into the very earth. And an immense dust cloud covered the drop ships and the airfield and was sweeping toward the golden domes. "Is there no end?" she said under her breath.

"Sorry?" Trisna Sahir said.

Katla beckoned. "Hurry! The airlock is close."

"Vishnu preserve us," Trisna said.

The street was becoming crammed with people who had the same idea. Terror-struck, they were clamoring to be let through the lock even though they weren't wearing EVA suits.

A trio of U.N.I.C. troopers were preventing anyone from entering. ICW's trained, they were telling everyone to go back to their homes, that for the time being only the military were allowed egress.

A woman shouted that she had no home to go back to, that it had sunk into the ground.

A man stalked up to a trooper and angrily demanded that he and his family be let out 'or else.' "Keeping us boxed will get us killed!" he railed, and others nodded and pressed forward.

"Enough!" The trooper fired a burst into the ground and the mob scampered back. "I won't tell you again! We are under orders not to let anyone use..." He stopped and pressed a finger to his temple. "Hold on!" he shouted and seemed to be listening. Straightening, he said, "New orders! We're to evacuate the colony! Right away!"

It was as if he were the little Dutch boy who once plugged a hole in a dyke with his finger---and then took his finger out. They all rushed forward at once. Men. Women. Children. The press drove the three troopers back against the inner door where they struggled to make room.

By then, Katla and Trisna were at the edge of the throng, with a barrier of pushing and shoving humanity between them and their salvation.

"How do we get through?" Trisna said.

A dark shadow fell across them.

Katla looked up in alarm. The dust cloud was enveloping the dome. A partial darkness descended. Screams broke out and people pushed one another and milled in confusion.

"Piotr, hold onto Trisna," Katla said, and the boy gulped and nodded. "Hold tight, do you understand? Whatever happens, don't let go of her."

"I won't," the boy said, his fear transparent.

"Trisna, stay close to my back," Katla said. "No matter what."

"What will you be doing?" she asked.

"What do you think?"

Katla shouldered into the press. Surprisingly, few resisted. It helped that many of them were gaping at the top of the dome and the dust. A man was blubbering and muttering to himself. She went around. A woman with two children had crouched with a jacket over their heads. She skirted them.

Katla pushed through a last knot of people and reached the airlock.

A trooper loomed, his ICW held crosswise over his chest.

"We want out," Katla said.

"The dust," the trooper said, indicating the cloud outside. "How far do you think you would get?"

"We're wearing suits. We can manage."

The trooper nodded. "I have no one I can send to protect you."

"We'll protect ourselves," Katla said, hefting her weapon. "Just let us out."

"You've got it." He moved toward the airlock panel.

"These poor people," Trisna said, looking over her shoulder. "They don't have suits. What will they do?"

"Poor us if we don't reach the drop ship," Katla said.

"Any word from Captain Rahn?"

"No," Katla said, her emotions welling. She had grown to care for that man, a lot. "Keep holding hands," she said. Only a few steps and they were at the inner door.

"Come on, come on," Katla said impatiently. She was under no illusion about how long the drop ships would wait. If things turned sour, if the ships were in danger, they would lift off---with or without the evacuees.

"What is the delay?" Trisna said.

"Maybe it won't open," Katla said. "Maybe the dust has gotten into the system."

"Don't say things like that."

Katla heard a hiss and the inner door moved. Anxiously, she pushed to try and speed things along but the door was too massive. She had to wait until it thunked to a stop. She and Trisna and the kids entered, and she pressed the speaker button. "We're in. You can pressurize."

The trooper's tinny voice replied, "Activating air exchange. Give it a minute."

Katla remembered that airlocks were one of Archard's few peeves. They operated so slowly, he once griped that he could write a book between the time the inner and outer doors opened. She'd grinned and told him it wasn't that bad.

She was wrong.

The cycling took forever. She fidgeted. She shifted her weight from leg to leg. She raised and lowered her ICW.

Just when she thought she couldn't bear the suspense another heartbeat, the outer door started to open.

"Finally!" Trisna exclaimed. "On to the drop ships!"

Yes, Katla thought. But first, they must make it past the Martians.

44

Captain Archard Rahn returned to the world of the living in fitful spurts. His consciousness flickered, succumbed to an abyss of emptiness, flickered anew. He became dimly aware of pressure on his body, as of a great weight. Then he passed out.

With a mild start, he came around yet again. He felt the weight, and a sharp pain in his hip, and a duller ache in his head. His eyelids fluttered, and for a few moments, he could have gone either way, down into the dark or up into the light. Struggling mightily, through sheer force of will he snapped his eyes open and sucked in a deep breath.

Disoriented, Archard tried to make sense of what he saw. The last thing he remembered was being struck down. He wondered if he had been moved while he was out. The stairwell had been brightly lit, but wherever he was now, there was hardly any light. He tried to turn his head to see better and couldn't because of the weight on top of him.

Directly under his faceplate, smearing it in places, was a reddish goo that made him think of pudding. Belatedly, he realized it was pulped Martian flesh. Only then did he remember falling onto he-knew-not-how-many dead Martians.

Other bodies must be on top of him.

He struggled, seeking to gauge how heavily he was pinned. He couldn't move either of his legs or his left arm but he was able to shift his right.

Encouraged, Archard braced his hands and legs and tried to rise. Nothing doing. Girding himself, he tried again, and this time rose perhaps a finger's width. The effort caused his head to pound and his hip to spike in greater pain in protest.

Pausing until the pain subsided, Archard listened for sounds from around him. Other than a faint drip of liquid---blood, possibly---he might as well be in a tomb. The silence was near total.

The fight must be over, he reasoned. The victors had moved on. The other troopers must have assumed he was dead. The

Martians, too. Or could it be that the creatures knew he was still alive and were waiting for him to reveal himself to pounce?

Archard waited, hoping the Martians would give themselves away. Except for the drip, the only sound was his own breathing.

A loud rumble from deep underground galvanized him into acting. He'd forgotten that the building was sinking. He had to get out of there before he was completely buried.

Girding himself, Archard heaved upward. The body or bodies on top of him gave a little. He heaved again, putting all his strength into it. The weight eased a fraction.

Archard pushed and pushed until he couldn't take the strain, and sank down. He rested, pushed, rested, pushed, so many times he lost count, until suddenly, as he strained to his utmost, the weight on top of him was gone.

Caked with sweat and gasping for breath, he pushed to his knees.

The stairwell was filled with the dead, troopers and BioMarines and Martians all intermixed, limbs askew, flesh and carapaces ruptured, organs spilled out, alien and human and hybrid blood mingling in pools.

No Martians were waiting for him. He had a dead BioMarine and several dead Martians to thank. They had fallen on top of him, shielding him from detection.

"Thank you," Archard gasped. Wearily, he rose. His ICW had been under him. Picking it up, he checked the magazine, then climbed over bodies until he reached the stairs.

As much as he would like to rest some more, time was of the essence.

Archard climbed, alert for Martians, fearing he might be the only human still breathing in the whole building.

Several landings up, he came on more bodies. A pitched battle had been fought and cost the lives of General Augusto's aide, Major Fogarty, as well as a lot of hybrids. The dead were three and four deep in places.

Archard didn't see any sign of the general.

Dreading that more Martians would show up, Archard took the stairs two at a bound.

Keying his personal frequency, Archard cleared his throat. "Katla? Can you hear me? Are you there?" She didn't answer. Either because he was too far underground or conditions topside were unfavorable or the unthinkable had happened to her.

Archard forced her from his mind and climbed faster. Yet another slaughter unfolded before him. The hybrids and troopers on point had put up a good fight but fared no better than the rest. He only saw a few dead BioMarines, which inclined him to believe that several might have escaped.

Other than an occasional rumbling, the building stayed stable until Archard reached the ground floor.

He was appalled to see that the main doors were blocked by a solid wall of dirt. Fear clawed at him, fear that U.N.I.C. headquarters might be completely buried. Returning to the stairwell, he climbed for the first floor and tried the exit door. It wouldn't budge. A glance out a window in a room told him why. More dirt.

"No," Archard prayed, and ran to the second floor. Entering another room, he dashed to a window and was elated to see the street and a patch of dome.

Just then the building gave another of its violent lurches, and the floor dipped under him.

Archard took a step back and cut loose with his ICW, stitching the pane to pieces. The glass fell away, clattering. Holding his arms and the ICW in front of his faceplate, he dived out. There was the sensation of falling. He came down hard on his side and tumbled a couple of meters and lay still, taking stock.

The ground under him was quaking. A horrendous grinding filled his ears.

Rising onto his elbows, Archard beheld an astounding sight. U.N.I.C. headquarters was sliding deeper into the earth. Dust spewed, and there were loud popping and crackling noises. When the racket finally stopped, only part of the upper floor and the roof were visible. The rest was buried.

Archard had gotten out in the nick of time. Pushing up, he slowly rose. His EVA suit was torn in a few places but the tears were minor and the suit was sealing. His ICW wasn't damaged.

Archard turned in a circle to get his bearings. The devastation was shocking. Two-thirds of the structures under Dome One were partially or completely buried. Dust from the sinkholes filled the air. Smoke rose from a number of fires. Screams and cries wafted from all quarters. People ran wildly, yelling and weeping. Martians scuttled after prey.

Above it all, the public address system was blaring an emergency message. "Attention colonists! We are evacuating Bradbury! You are instructed to report to the drop ships at the airfield for immediate extraction!"

Archard broke into a jog. If Katla was anywhere, it would be there. He was going to find her and get her safely off-planet---or die trying.

45

KLL-12 reached the end of Asimov Avenue and turned onto Dick Street. On all sides, buildings were shaking and sinking, making tremendous grinding noises as they slowly disappeared. The humans were in a state of panic.

"I still can't raise KLL-1," KLL-13 said, swiping a hand across her gore-streaked forehead.

"We are on our own from here on out," KLL-12 said.

"Hold on," KLL-15 said. He had been trailing a little behind but now he caught up. "What's your plan?"

"To reach the drop ships and take one up to the fleet in orbit."

"What about the rest of our unit?" KLL-15 said.

"So far as we know, we're the only BioMarines left," KLL-12 said.

Sudden scratching issued from a partially sunken residence and he shifted to watch the windows.

"You don't know that for certain," KLL-15 said. "Just because we can't raise them doesn't mean some of them aren't still alive."

"He's right," KLL-13 said.

"We're BioMarines," KLL-15 flatly declared. "We don't abandon our own."

"Booyah," KLL-13 said and grinned.

"Are you two done?" KLL-12 said. "If you want to go search for them, go. But look around you first. The colony is doomed. It will soon be overrun. The Martians will kill everyone. Including you."

"We can't just desert our own," KLL-15 insisted.

"And what about the humans?" KLL-13 said.

"What about them?" KLL-12 said. "They brought this on themselves. Their leaders knew this planet was inhabited. They thought they could colonize it under the Martians' very nose. They were wrong. Now they're paying for their arrogance."

"Doesn't matter," KLL-15 said. "We are sworn to protect them wherever and however necessary."

"We were conditioned to protect them," KLL-12 amended, "whether we want to or not."

"Here we go again," KLL-13 said tiredly.

KLL-12 faced them. "Then consider this. Seniority in our unit is based on the order of our creation, yes? Even though we are all essentially alike?"

"Except for our personalities," KLL-13 said and winked.

"As the first of us, KLL-1 was our leader. KLL-2 our second-in-command."

"So?" KLL-15 said.

"So since twelve comes before thirteen and fifteen, that makes me senior here. And I order the two of you to follow me to the drop ships and escape this madhouse before it is too late."

They looked at each other and KLL-13 said, "He has a point."

"I still don't like running from a fight," KLL-15.

The front windows in the residence shattered, disgorging Martians one after the other. Fanning out as they came, the crabs scrabbled toward the BioMarines.

"Be careful what you wish for," KLL-13 said to KLL-15.

Then there was no time for talk. The Martians were on them.

KLL-12 fought with a ferocity born of desperation. He refused to die. He enjoyed being alive. Whether created in a test-tube or natural-born, life was precious. Those who didn't think so were fools.

Unlike the humans, he had no belief in an afterlife. No assurance whatsoever that some part of him would survive were his body to be slain. "This" was it, and he would fight for his right to go on breathing with every iota of his being.

So he slew in a berserker fury while dodging and ducking and sidestepping with a speed the Martians were hard-pressed to match.

Out of the corner of an eye, he saw KLL-13 rip a creature in half and secretly delighted in her bloodlust.

KLL-15 was doing his part, too. He had plowed into the Martians like a ship into a wave, meeting them head-on, his lethality a testimony to how he had survived the battle in the stairwell.

Twenty, thirty, forty Martians had been dispatched, and the ground littered with twitching limbs and ruptured carapaces when the flow of creatures out of the house stopped.

Breathing heavily, KLL-13 laughed and said, "We did it!"

"We've done nothing," KLL-12 said. "There are a million more to take their place."

"You're a real buzzkill, you know that?"

"Let's go," KLL-12 said, and started off in prodigious leaps and bounds thanks to Mars' lesser gravity.

"Where to?" KLL-13 asked, matching him. "The main airlock?"

"A secondary," KLL-12 said. "The main will be jammed with humans trying to escape."

"You think of everything," she said sweetly.

Most of the people they passed were too distraught or too terror-struck to pay much notice. A few called out and raised their hands in appeal.

"They want our help," KLL-15 said.

KLL-12 ignored him. For their own sake, they must resist their conditioning. They must think for themselves and not let their common sense be overpowered by whatever the humans had done to them.

"I don't know if I can abandon them," KLL-15 said. "It doesn't feel right."

"You will follow my orders, soldier," KLL-12 declared. "Stay with us, you hear?"

Above them, the golden dome had darkened. A gigantic dust cloud was descending and would soon envelop the entire dome.

More Martians were appearing and attacking humans at random.

And all the while, the buildings continued to sink. Like so many half-buried headstones, they lent the scene the aspect of a macabre cemetery.

KLL-12 turned onto Kline Street. Ahead was the airlock. Several troopers were trying to hold back a mob clamoring for turns.

"Look at them," KLL-13 said. "The poor things."

"Our great makers," KLL-12 said. He stopped short of the squabbling press of humanity and bellowed, "Out of the way! Official business!"

The humans turned and gaped and were quick to move aside for the towering newcomers. The few who didn't, KLL-12 only had to flick a claw and they stepped back.

One of the troopers snapped to attention. "Sir!" he said. "You're with the general, yes?"

"We are part of his special unit," KLL-12 said. "And we need out."

"Right away, sir. You take priority over anyone else." The soldier turned to the control panel. "You're so big, it will be cramped. I don't think all three of you will fit."

"KLL-13 and KLL-15, you go first," KLL-12 ordered. He waited while they entered and the airlock cycled.

The humans had grown quiet, cowed by his presence.

As the inner door started to hiss open again, KLL-12 bent over the trooper at the panel. "You have done me a favor, soldier," he said quietly, "and I will do you one."

"Sir?"

"General Augusto is dead. The colony is about to fall. I recommend that you and your friends vacate your post and get to a drop ship."

The trooper blanched and swallowed. "Dear God," he whispered.

Staying bent, KLL-12 eased into the airlock. He didn't know why he had just done that. Facing the outer door, he endured the wait necessitated by the change in pressure.

KLL-13 and KLL-15 were crouched down, their mouths and gills working in conjunction to enable their lungs to endure the Martian atmosphere, their hands raised to their faces to ward off the dust.

"It's a nightmare out here," KLL-13 said and coughed.

"It's a nightmare everywhere," KLL-12 said. He motioned for them to stand. "Let's hustle before the Martians do what they should have done before they launched their assault."

"What's that?" KLL-13 said.

"Destroy the drop ships so we can't escape."

46

Private Everett and Private Keller swung their ICW's toward the sound coming out of the dust. Everett was sure it must be a Martian until a bloody hand---or, rather, a hand in an EVA suit covered with blood---groped the trench rim and waved in the air as if in appeal.

"It's one of ours!" Keller exclaimed. Lowering her weapon, she chugged up the slope.

Everett went with her to cover her.

"Careful!" Sergeant Kline yelled.

"You heard him!" Captain Ferris hollered, sounding as if she were in terrible agony. "We can't afford to lose anyone."

"I hear that, ma'am," Everett said.

It was a young trooper.

Kneeling, Keller gripped his hand, saying, "It's all right. We've got you."

His suit was a mess. Fortunately, the seals had held. And his left leg was bent at an angle no leg was ever meant to.

"Thank God," he gasped.

Everett had his sensors at max and his eyes glued to his helmet's holo display. Not that the sensors would do much good with all the dust.

"I'm hurt," the young trooper wheezed. "Bad."

"We can see that," Private Keller said. "I don't suppose you can stand?"

"Sorry," the trooper said, weakly shaking his head. "Name's Griffin. Maser detail. We were overrun."

At the bottom of the trench, Sergeant Kline said, "What's the holdup? We have to beat feet."

"Your story will have to wait," Keller told Griffin. Sliding her free arm under his, she said, "Lean on me and I'll get you to the drop ships."

"Why not to the dome?" he asked.

"Bradbury is being evacuated. The order is being broadcast on all frequencies," Keller enlightened him. "Now quiet. We have a lot of ground to cover."

"Private Everett, take point," Sergeant Kline barked.

Sliding down, Everett nodded and dashed past the noncom and the captain. Only then did it occur to him that he was the only one with their hands free and able to quickly engage the enemy should they be attacked.

"Don't get too far ahead," Captain Ferris said.

As if Everett would. The dust was so thick, the sky so dark, anything beyond two meters was lost to view. Every nerve tingling, he cautiously advanced.

The lull in the battle puzzled him. He would have thought the Martians would keep coming until every last Earther lay dead. Or was the dust inhibiting their senses, too? He knew so little about them. For that matter, as was now abundantly clear, Earth's leaders didn't know much, either, or Bradbury wouldn't be on the verge of falling.

His helmet crackled. "Private Everett, can you hear me?" Captain Ferris said.

"Affirmative, sir," Everett replied.

"Sitrep."

"Dust, dust, and more dust," Everett said. "If it wasn't for my compass, I wouldn't be sure I'm going the right way."

"You should come to the next maser emplacement soon. Stay frosty."

"As icing," Everett said.

"What?"

"Nothing, sir." Everett rounded a bend and stopped cold. Before him rose the emplacement, a vague shape in the settling dust. He moved closer. The maser and its housing had been reduced to rubble. Venturing amid the debris, he spied bodies. All of them had had their arms and legs torn off and placed next to their torso. And every single one, the head was missing.

Everett had forgotten about the Martian fondness for trophies. Never in a million years would he have imagined an alien species would resort to primitive headhunting.

He would be damned if they'd get his.

"Everett? Talk to me," Captain Ferris said.

"I'm there, ma'am. A lot of dead but no sign of the Martians."

"Stay put. We'll join you in a bit."

"Yes, ma'am."

Stepping over a torso with a gaping hole where the abdomen should be, Everett leaned on a section of broken maser and peered ahead. Call it wishful thinking, but the dust appeared to be thinning a little.

Everett switched to the colony's primary broadcast frequency and heard the evacuation order being repeated in an endless loop. He tried the U.N.I.C.'s military band and picked up scattered chatter too garbled to understand. He wondered if the Martians were jamming them somehow.

"Private Everett? Where are you?"

Everett turned.

Sergeant Kline and Captain Ferris were surveying the carnage. Behind them, Private Keller was doing her best to keep Private Griffin on his feet and had slung her ICW so she could use both arms to support him.

Everett couldn't help thinking that if a swarm struck, they were sitting ducks.

"Still no sign of the creatures?" Captain Ferris asked.

"Strangely enough, no," Everett said.

Ferris frowned and shook her helmet. "I don't get it. Where did they go? They had us dead to rights."

"Ever hear of a gift horse?" Sergeant Kline said.

"I'm not complaining," Captain Ferris said, and groaned. "The shape I'm in, I'll take every miracle that comes our way."

Private Keller broke in with, "Shouldn't we keep going, ma'am? Private Griffin, here, isn't light."

"Everett," Captain Ferris said. "Head out. But stay with us this time."

Nodding, Everett swung around the housing and ascended a short grade. He could see about three meters. The dust obscured a short plain. Beyond that lay the airfield.

Captain Ferris coughed and said, "All we have to do is cross that open area and we'll be at the drop ships."

"Is that all?" Private Keller said.

"Chin up," Captain Ferris said. "It's not too much to expect another miracle, is it?"

No one answered her.

47

General Constantine Augusto was in a state of shock. As he was swiftly borne through dark tunnels by alien creatures straight from a lunatic's nightmare, he struggled to retain a grip on his own sanity.

To be captured by the enemy, to have his meticulously laid plans be thrown into chaos, to fail so spectacularly, was almost more than he could bear. An urge to scream came over him and he opened his mouth to give vent to the horror---and closed it again.

No. He refused to show such blatant weakness. He was a soldier. He was U.N.I.C. He was a supreme commander, no less. His whole life had been devoted to the art of control. To controlling others, and controlling himself. If he couldn't exercise control now, during the most dire crisis of his life, he put the lie to all that had gone before.

Closing his eyes, General Augusto willed himself to stay calm, to not let the devastating series of events cripple his ability to reason. So long as he stayed sharp, there was always a chance he could extricate himself from this impossible predicament. Perhaps he could reason with the Martians. How that was even possible when he couldn't communicate with them was a problem to be solved when the opportunity arose. In the meantime, he must stay calm.

Augusto couldn't tell much about his surroundings other than that the tunnel walls were composed of hard rock. The constant scritching and scratching the creatures made gnawed at his nerves. He surmised, based on the slope of the tunnel floor, that he was being taken far underground.

Now and again, Augusto glimpsed junctions and branches and open areas. He also caught sight of other creatures, some many times larger than the crabs carrying him.

The descent seemed to take hours, although it could have been much less.

Suddenly, the tunnel widened and brightened until it was comparable to Martian twilight. The light source was a phosphorescent fungus, or so he imagined the growth to be, high on the walls and ceiling.

The creatures came to a stop.

Twisting his neck, General Augusto looked down and gasped. They were poised on the brink of a vast drop-off. For a few harrowing seconds, he thought the things were going to throw him down it, but no, they scrabbled to a stone bridge linked to what could only be called an avenue bracketed by giant columns.

Martians of all kind were all over. Each and every one stopped what they were doing to raise their eye stalks and stare as he was carried past.

General Augusto's skin crawled at the proximity of so many otherworldly abominations. "I hate these things," he said out loud.

The multifaceted eyes belonging to the creature holding his right arm materialized centimeters from his face and fixed on his.

"What, you ugly bastard?" General Augusto said and laughed. It felt good to insult the thing, to show he wasn't completely helpless.

Its eye stalks swung away.

Structures reared. The avenue had brought them to a large plateau crowded with buildings. Their destination appeared to be the tallest.

General Augusto girded himself for the worst. He figured there must be a purpose to his capture. Why else had they taken him alive when they could easily have ripped his head off as they did with everyone else? He wondered if they indulged in torture. Or maybe---and the thought jarred him---they took some humans alive to *eat* them. For all he knew, they liked to chow down on raw human flesh.

Entry to the tall structure was through a wide doorway in the shape of a triangle. Once inside, General Augusto beheld a huge lobby bustling with activity. Recesses in the walls contained what he took to be sculptures, but they were unlike any a human mind could conceive, consisting of configurations based on an aesthetic sense beyond mortal ken.

Instead of stairs, the Martians relied on ramps. Augusto stopped counting at twenty. He guessed that he was being whisked to the very pinnacle, and he wasn't mistaken. His captors finally entered a broad chamber where various kinds of Martians were arrayed in orderly rows facing a wide basalt dais, empty at the moment.

The eye stalks of every Martians turned toward him as he was carried to the base of the dais and unceremoniously dumped onto his back. The four creatures that had brought him stepped to either side and faced him, their grippers spread menacingly. The threat was clear.

Rolling over, General Augusto slowly sat up. He ached all over from being carried for so long. Amazingly, his uniform was intact. Neither his jacket sleeves nor his pant legs were torn where the creatures had seized him. Their grippers looked to be awkward and clumsy, yet the creatures were capable of great delicacy.

Augusto heard a scuttling sound behind him and started to turn. He froze when he saw that one of the huge blue warriors, the kind that resembled lobsters, had come up and was studying him.

"Are you my counterpart?" Augusto said to show he wasn't intimidated. "Are you a general, like me?"

The blue creature lowered its eyes so they were level with his.

"You don't scare me," General Augusto said. "None of you do."

The blue warrior and every other Martian abruptly turned toward the dais. Or, rather, toward an opening past it, through which a yellow Martian was entering. Two others of the same kind followed it.

"Let me guess," General Augusto blustered. "You're the big brains."

The trio ascended a ramp to the dais and spread out with the first one in the middle. Taller than the others, its mushroom-shaped carapace bigger, it came to the edge and stared at Augusto.

"Get on with it, bastard."

Nothing happened. The Martians stayed motionless except for the ceaseless waving of their eye stalks.

General Augusto coughed. His mouth was dry and his palms were sweating. He would give anything to have an ICW and a dozen grenades so he could fight his way out.

How long went by, he couldn't say. He glanced at the blue warrior and then at their evident leader. "Are you just going to stand there? Do something, damn you."

The Martians went on imitating statues.

Just when Augusto thought he couldn't stand it anymore, there was a commotion, and into the chamber hurried a dozen or so of the small reddish-pink caste, the crabs. To his astonishment, they had brought several items with them; a computer with a large screen, a touch pad, a Wi-Fi unit to connect them, and a military grade battery pack for power.

"What the hell?" General Augusto blurted.

The Martians knew just what they were doing. They placed the computer on the dais, facing him. They hooked up the Wi-Fi and the power pack, and then one of them---the top of its carapace bearing the mark of a long scar---used the tip of a leg to press the power button on the battery pack. The screen flared to electronic life. The same creature then turned toward Augusto and squatted with the touchpad on the ground in front of it.

"What in God's name *is* this?" Augusto said to the yellow leader. He refused to accept the evidence of his own eyes; that the Martians had figured out how to use Earth tech.

The yellow leader and the red creature were looking at one another. Augusto had a sense that they were in contact, somehow, a sense confirmed when the yellow Martian gestured and the red crab dipped its eye stalks to the touch pad and lightly tapped the pad with the tip of a front leg.

On the computer screen, *Hello, General Augusto* appeared.

Shocked to his marrow, General Augusto gaped.

The Martian tapped some more. *"Cat got your tongue?"*

Nearly numb with disbelief, General Augusto exclaimed, "This can't be happening. I must be going crazy."

"On the contrary, General," the Martian typed. *"Please compose yourself. We have a lot to discuss of supreme importance to the human race."*

"What do you know of my kind?" General Augusto said sarcastically.

"More than you might imagine, General," the creature typed. *"You see, I was human once."*

48

Dr. Katla Dkany had the awful feeling that she and Trisna and the children had been walking in circles for who-knew-how-long.

The dust was to blame.

Once out of the airlock, Katla had made straight for the airfield. Or so she thought. On a clear day, they would have reached it in less than ten minutes. Twice that long passed, and no airfield. Hampered by the dust, they were wandering helter-skelter.

Normally, EVA suits incorporated GPS and compass functions, but the suits they took from the emergency shelter were older models, unable to link with the colony's satellite to establish their exact location. And their compass readings were all over the place.

Katla had lost all sense of direction. Coming to a stop, she bowed her head and closed her eyes.

"Are you all right?" Trisna asked.

"A little tired, is all."

"We should be there soon, shouldn't we?"

"Soon," Katla said, inwardly praying, *please let it be so.* Bending, she placed a hand on Piotr's shoulder. "How are you holding up?"

"I'm scared," the boy said.

"Me too," Behulah echoed from her perch on her mother's chest.

"Hang in there," Katla reassured them. "It won't be long." Unfolding, she set off as if she knew exactly where she was going, when in fact they might be well past the airfield and in the middle of nowhere. That they hadn't blundered onto the Martians was an inevitability waiting to happen.

"I think I saw something," Trisna said worriedly.

Stopping, Katla gazed about them into the pea soup. "Where?"

Trisna pointed. "There. Low to the ground."

Please no, Katla thought. She squatted, raising her ICW as she did. Inadvertently, she saved her life.

Out of the dust rushed a red Martian, right into her weapon's muzzle. Moving incredibly fast, it was almost on her when she squeezed the trigger in startled reflex and blew its frontal ridge to bits. It sprawled at her feet even as the dust disgorged another scuttling toward Trisna and the children.

Behulah screamed.

Katla spun to fire but someone beat her to it. High-velocity rounds stitched the creature from end to end, collapsing it in midleap. A third creature appeared, and hesitated, waving its grippers as if unsure who to attack first. Another burst cut it down.

Turning, Katla almost shouted for joy. Troopers were appearing out of the gloom. Her elation was cut short by the realization that two of them were hurt and being supported by others. It was the fifth man who had saved them. There was something familiar about the features behind the faceplate.

He came up, smiling. "Howdy again, Doc. We sure do have a knack for running into trouble, don't we?"

"Private Everett!" Katla exclaimed, and forgetting herself, threw her arms around him.

"It's good to see you and Ms. Sahir, too," Private Everett said. "But I'd best keep my arms free in case there are more of those critters."

"Oh. Sorry." Katla self-consciously released him and stepped back. "We're just so happy to see you. We're lost."

"We are?" Trisna said.

A woman with a captain's insignia on her EVA suit, leaning on a sergeant whose features were also familiar, spoke up, "Private Everett, you know these people?"

"Fellow survivors from Wellsville and New Meridian, sir," the Kentuckian said.

Katla leaned toward the sergeant. "Sergeant Kline, is that you?"

"In person, Doc," the noncom said.

"How did you find us?" Katla said in amazement. "How did you even know we were out here?"

"We didn't," the officer said. "I'm Captain Ferris, by the way. We're on our way to the airfield. Our infrared sensors picked you up." She glanced at the dead Martians. "Just in time, it seems."

"We're looking for the airfield, too," Katla said. "Can we join you?"

"Need you even ask?" Ferris said. "Fall in behind me. And keep your weapon handy."

"Gladly," Katla said. As she moved to comply, she paused next to Everett. "Have you heard anything from Archard?"

"No, ma'am," Private Everett said. "Last I knew, he was at HQ."

"Head out," Captain Ferris said. "Those drop ships aren't going to wait around forever. Everett, you're on point again."

"Yes, ma'am."

Mixed emotions flooded through Katla. Palpable relief that the troopers increased their chances of reaching the airfield safely, and deep dismay that Archard might be dead back inside the dome, and she had no way of knowing.

"Be alive, damn you," she whispered.

49

General Constantine Augusto's mind reeled. His reality had come crashing down around him in shards of incredulity. The sheer rank horror of the astounding revelation the Martian had just made, and what it implied, defied all logic. "You can't be what you claim," he exclaimed.

The red Martian did more tapping, moving the tip of its limb with a fluidity that was almost as disconcerting as its ability to use Earth tech so expertly.

"General Augusto, permit me to introduce myself. In my previous life, I was known as Levlin Winslow, Chief Administrator at New Meridian."

"No!" Augusto gasped. He refused to believe it.

"I was taken captive by the Martians, just as you have been. They tore off my head, just as they have done to nearly every Earther they encounter."

"No!" Augusto said again.

"Haven't you wondered why they do that? Why only the heads? The answer is simple. The head is the seat of our consciousness. And through a process I can't begin to comprehend, through science far beyond anything on Earth, they transferred my consciousness into the body you see before you."

Augusto vigorously shook his head. "No, no, no."

The computer screen flashed anew. *"I was in denial, too, at first. I nearly went mad. You have no idea what it was like to wake up in this body."*

"God," Augusto said.

"Eventually, the Martians brought me out of myself," the creature tapped. *"I was given a new name, Kralun, and I acquired a mate…"*

"You what?"

"…and I learned to immerse my consciousness in the Unity."

"The what?"

"In short, General Augusto," the former Earthman typed, *"I was made into a Martian. Not just in body. In mind and heart and soul. I have given myself over to the Source of All."*

General Augusto couldn't take any more. "Hold on, hold on! You're going too fast! None of this makes sense. I never met Levlin Winslow but I know who he was. And you claim to be him?"

"I was born in Chicago. My wife's name was Gladys. I was a career politician. My U.N. identification number…"

"Wait," General Augusto said. "What was that business about something called the Unity and the Source?"

"The Martians, General, are a deeply spiritual species."

Augusto gazed at the abominations that filled the chamber. "You've got to be kidding."

"In battle, they try to kill as few of their enemies as possible. The rest they convert, as they did me and many of the people from New Meridian and Wellsville."

"You're saying most of the colonists are alive?"

"I'm saying that they are as I am," the creature tapped. *"A Gryghr. And before you ask, that is my caste. The blue warrior behind you is a Hryghr. Our castes are based on our function."*

"What about that thing?" General Augusto said, pointing at the tall yellow creature at the front of the dais.

"He is an Aryghr. A leader. As are those other two behind him." Levlin Winslow or Kralun or whatever the creature called itself stopped tapping and its stalk eyes rose. *"Do you recognize him?"*

"Why should I?" General Augusto said.

"Because he is the one you thought you had captured. But who, in fact, let himself be taken prisoner so that he could direct our attack on Bradbury from within. And to take you prisoner, too, of course."

"Captain Rahn was right about that thing, then," General Augusto said, more to himself than to the crab.

"Archard Rahn? I knew him at New Meridian. I would have thought he had enough sense to be back on Earth by now. Not that that would do him any good."

"What are you talking about?"

Levlin Winslow, now called Kralun, shifted toward the yellow leader and was motionless for all of a minute. Finally, the former administrator stirred and faced him.

"What were you doing? Communicating somehow?" Augusto said.

"We can all commune one with one another by immersing our sentience in the group consciousness of the Unity" the creature typed. *"The closest Earth analogy as to how would be telepathy."*

"Impossible."

"How can you be so naïve after all you have witnessed?" Kralun paused. *"I was asking if it is permissible to answer your question about Earth."*

"I'm more interested to learn what they intend to do with me."

"That should be obvious." Kralun raised a gripper and pointed it at himself.

Augusto felt sick inside at the idea of being turned into a hideous crab.

"Your conversion is key to our overall strategy," Kralun typed on. *"With you on our side to advise our leaders, our war can enter its next phase."*

"What are you on about now? What phase?"

"Why, our invasion of Earth, of course."

50

Captain Archard Rahn came within sight of the main airlock, expecting to find it jammed with troopers and civilians eager to reach the airfield and escape the chaos. Instead, he beheld a tangled carpet of bodies for a block around, mostly human but more than a few Martian. The humans were all missing their heads.

Drawing up short, Archard raised his ICW. He boosted his motion sensors to the max but his holo display only registered twitching limbs. His infrared showed many of the human bodies were still warm.

So where had the Martians gotten to that killed them?

Archard warily went nearer. He tried his commlink, U.N.I.C.'s general frequency, and requested that any personnel within range respond. All he heard was static.

Outside the dome, the dust had brought about a preternatural darkness. There could be a Martian swarm a stone's throw from the nanosheath and Archard wouldn't know it.

From out of the depths of a building sliding into the ground came a scream of mortal terror that ended in a whimper.

Archard's first instinct was to go to their aid. He was a trooper, after all. Protecting colonists was his primary mission. But to plunge into that sinking structure would be the equivalent of throwing his life away.

He must live to reach Earth. Get the word out that the natives on the Red Planet were ruthless beyond belief and no amount of force thrown at them would make them agree to human colonization.

Mars, Archard grimly reflected, had won the war of the worlds. The only thing for the Earthers still alive was to reach the fleet and head for home as fast as their EmDrives would take them.

Picking his way over the dead, he was almost to the airlock when a noise from a side street down the block warned him that company was coming.

Into the open scuttled a pack of twenty or so crustoids, their eye stalks waving, their grippers in an attack posture.

"Crabs, crabs, and more crabs," Archard muttered as he fed a frag grenade into the ICW's firing tube. The control light went from red to green and he tilted the ICW for the right trajectory.

The Martians spotted him and charged to the attack.

Archard triggered the frag. The moment the tube whooshed, he fed in another, and fired again. Then a third. The first explosion blasted the nearest, the second crumpled creatures in the middle of the pack, the third blistered survivors trying to scatter. Only five were left but that was more than enough as they spread out and scrabbled with incredible speed to reach him. Backpedaling, he switched to full auto and stitched the fastest and another in its crustoid face when it jumped at his.

That left three. They were smart and came at him from different directions, unbelievably quick. He couldn't possibly drop them all before they reached him but he would try. He took aim at one to his left and riddled it and spun to shoot another on the right just in time to see a BioMarine come out of nowhere, seize the Martian by its legs, and tear the creature apart.

The last one vaulted at Archard and he cored its shell.

Her hand to her side, the BioMarine mustered a smile. "Nicely done."

"Thanks for the assist," Archard said.

"Booyah," she said, coming over.

"You're hurt."

"I'll live," she replied. "I'm KLL-10. You're Captain Rahn. I saw you with the general."

"How many others of…" Archard was going to say "your kind" but instead said, "…your unit are left?"

"Would that I knew," KLL-10 said. "I became separated from the rest in the stairwell. The Martians pulled me into a tunnel. How I broke free I will never know. There were so many."

"You made it topside. That's what counts," Archard said.

"If you say so."

"Are you all right?"

"Beyond the obvious?" KLL-10 said, moving her hand enough for him to see the full extent of her wound. It was deep, and she had bled a lot. "I have been trying to reach others in my unit on my commlink but all I get is static."

"Same here."

"I can't be the only one of us to make it out," KLL-10 said.

"I just can't."

Archard became aware of the continued blaring of the evacuation order. "You hear that? I'm on my way to the airfield. You should come with me."

KLL-10 gazed sadly about. "I guess there's nothing more we can do here. Although I'm not supposed to abandon humans in need."

Although he was unsure which of them outranked the other, Archard said, "Consider it an order."

KLL-10 smiled. "Thank you, Captain. Yes, I will accompany you. Perhaps together we can live long enough to make it off this wretched planet."

"I hear that," Archard said.

51

General Constantine Augusto had never heard anything so preposterous. "You're looney, Winslow or Kralun or whatever the hell you call yourself. There's no way the Martians can attack Earth. They don't have spacecraft."

Kralun tapped on his pad and the screen displayed, "*An entire fleet waits for us in orbit.*"

"Our fleet," General Augusto said in contempt. "Which the Martians don't know how to operate. Not even turncoats like you can. You were in admin, not a space jockey. It takes special training. Years of it. Which you don't have. Our fleet is where you can't ever reach it."

"*The drop ships can,*" Kralun typed.

General Augusto was losing his patience. "Again," he said angrily, "It takes a pilot to fly one. And I gave specific orders that the drop ship pilots were to stay at the airfield. Unless your crustacean friends have captured one, there's no way you're getting off this planet."

"*We have not captured a pilot, no,*" Kralun typed. "*Even if we had, the conversion process takes a considerable while. The wisest recourse for us, therefore, is for your pilots to fly us to the spacecraft in orbit.*"

"As if they would," General Augusto sneered.

"*They would if they were unaware we were on board their drop ships,*" Kralun typed. "*Are you familiar with the concept of stowaways, General?*"

Augusto glared. The thing was mocking him.

"*At this very moment, an evacuation is underway,*" Kralun tapped. "*Any humans still alive are fleeing to the airfield. And we are taking particular pains to ensure some of them reach it.*"

"No," Augusto gasped as the full scope of the Martian strategy sank in.

"*Yes. Presently, the drop ships will presently lift off, achieve orbit, and dock with the spacecraft that brought them.*" Kralun's prismatic eyes seemed to gleam with triumph. *"Taking a lot of us with them."*

"Hold on," General Augusto said. "You've outsmarted yourselves. Our drop ships and our spaceships are pressurized. Fourteen pounds per square inch, exactly like on Earth."

"So?"

"So what is it here on Mars? Barely a pound per square inch?" Augusto laughed. "You'll be crushed like the bugs you are."

"You might be interested to learn that while your species is so fragile it can't survive on our world's atmosphere without special suits, our hard shells enable us to survive under Earth's pressure quite well."

"But you need to breathe, don't you?" Augusto said. "Our air isn't the same as yours. You'd suffocate."

"Yes, Earth's atmosphere is seventy-eight percent nitrogen and twenty-one percent oxygen, while ours is ninety-five percent carbon dioxide and two percent nitrogen," Kralun typed, and his eyes lifted to Augusto. *"Guess which we breathe?"*

"The carbon dioxide?"

"No. It is mainly a surface gas. And in case you haven't noticed, the Martians are an underground race."

General Augusto was struck speechless by the implications.

"Our scientists believe we can survive in Earth's atmosphere quite well. The greater gravity might be an issue. But we will adapt, as the Unity always does."

Augusto shook his head. "There's a flaw in your reasoning. How many can you possibly smuggle onto the drop ships? Dozens? Maybe a few hundred? Earth's population is in the billions. You won't stand a prayer."

"That would be true if our numbers stayed static. But you see. Those billions you allude to will be converted, as I was, and most of the other colonists."

"Hold on," Augusto said. "You told me that the Martians transferred your consciousness into that red crab, right?"

"Yes."

"They did the same with the other colonists? A Martian body for each one?"

"Yes."

General Augusto smiled smugly. "Where are all the Martian bodies going to come from for those billions of Earthers? Are you going to wave a magic wand, and presto, there they are?"

"*That is our secret, General,*" Kralun typed.

"Eh?"

"*Never forget, General. Our science is vastly superior to yours. Especially our biological sciences.*"

"You're bluffing."

On the computer screen appeared the reply, "*Am I?*"

"God, no," Augusto said.

Kralun continued tapping. "*Your own conversion is about to commence. I envy you the joy in store when you experience the Unity for the first time.*"

Before Augusto could so much as blink, the four creatures who had brought him to the chamber sprang and seized his arms and legs. "Wait!" he shouted.

Kralun waggled a gripper as if waving goodbye.

Twisting and thrashing, Augusto sought to break loose. But he was helpless in their grasp. They bore him out of the chamber and down a different series of ramps to a rock-hewn corridor many levels below. Entering a room, they halted.

Sheer terror rippled down General Augusto's spine.

The room was lined with shelves filled with rows of severed human heads, some so recently added that they dripped blood.

In the center were rock slabs on which a strange apparatus bubbled and hissed, attended by brown Martians unlike any General Augusto had seen. As he looked on in bewilderment, one of the brown creatures came toward him.

"I refuse, you hear me?" Augusto railed. "I won't let you turn me into a monster!"

Paying him no heed, the brown Martian bent and reached for his head.

52

Captain Archard Rahn was sure it wasn't his imagination. The dust was thinning.

By his estimation, he and KLL-10 were about halfway to the airfield. They were going slowly, warily, every sensor in his EVA suit at max.

So far, the only Martians they came across were dead ones. A lot of dead humans, too, soldiers for the most part but too many civilians as well.

Archard couldn't believe his string of calamities. He'd survived the attack on New Meridian, the first colony to fall, and managed to reach the second, Wellsville, only to be forced to go through the whole ordeal again. Not satisfied with putting him through hell twice, Fate had brought the third colony crashing down around his helmet. Or, rather, sinking down.

"If I didn't have bad luck," he muttered, "I wouldn't have any luck at all."

"Sorry?" KLL-10 said.

"Nothing," Archard said. "Whining to myself, is all."

"A human trait BioMarines do not share." She was still holding her hand to her side. The bleeding had stopped but she was clearly in terrible pain and trying hard not to let her wound slow her. "We are psychologically conditioned to maintain an even emotional keel. Most of us are usually very upbeat, as you would say."

Knowing they shouldn't be making small talk when they could be attacked at any moment, Archard nonetheless said, "Most?"

"There is one of us who grumbles now and then. He isn't satisfied with the status quo."

Archard was about to ask which one of her unit it was when his sensors pinged. Halting, he increased the magnification factor on his holo display. "I'm picking up motion and heat sigs." He counted nine. "Human."

"Where?"

"Twenty meters to the northeast."

"We should join them," KLL-10 suggested. "Increase our chances of success."

"We can catch up if we hurry," Archard said. "Are you sure you're up to it?"

KLL-10 smiled. "Thank you for your concern. I'll manage, yes. Wounds this big, our healing factors take a while to repair. I am feeling stronger than I did earlier."

"Let's hustle, then."

Archard was a good ten meters from the clustered group when he distinguished their outlines. They were apparently aware of his approach and had stopped.

"This is Captain Irene Ferris," his helmet suddenly blared. "Identify yourself."

"Captain Archard Rahn," he responded, "with BioMarine KLL-10."

Archard heard a squeal in his earphones and one of the figures came running toward him with its arms outspread. His personal frequency burst with a shriek that nearly ruptured his eardrums.

"Archard! Oh, Archard!"

Then Dr. Katla Dkany had her arms around him and was squeezing him with her faceplate brushing his. The tears that formed in the corners of her eyes moved him deeply.

"Katla," Archard said huskily.

"I thought you were dead," Katla said.

"Not yet, but Mars is trying its best," Archard joked, aware that others were converging. He recognized some of them but not the wounded captain who couldn't walk on her own.

"Captain Rahn? I'm Ferris. I take it you already know Dr. Dkany. This other woman is Trisna Sahir, with her little girl Behulah, and the boy is…."

"Piotr Zabinski," Archard finished for her. "He's been with us since the beginning."

"Yes, well, you might also know some of the troopers," Captain Ferris said, gesturing. "Sergeant Kline and Privates Keller, Everett and Griffin. Two of us are hurt." She stared at Archard's insignia. "How long have you had your bars?"

"Seven years, four months."

"Six years, eleven months," Captain Ferris said. "Which puts you in charge." She sounded relieved. "What are our orders, sir?"

"What else?" Archard replied. "We get to the drop ships and off this godforsaken world."

"We hear that, Captain," Private Everett said.

Archard formed them up with the wounded in the middle, Katla helping Ferris and Keller continuing to support Griffin. He had Everett and Kline bring up the rear while he took point with KLL-10.

His mood brightened considerably. Katla meant a lot to him. For that matter, he was also fond of Trisna Sahir and the Kentuckian, whom he had known since New Meridian.

Archard reminded himself not to let his mind drift. Until they lifted off, they were in as much danger as ever.

The dust had settled enough that the large hanger in the distance was visible. Figuring reception might have improved, Archard tried the U.N.I.C. frequency again and was pleasantly surprised when someone answered.

"Captain Rahn? This is Lieutenant Ulla Burroughs. Do you copy?"

"Roger that, Lieutenant," Archard said. "I'm with ten others, en route to the airfield. Where are you? Do you require assistance?"

"I'm there already with Private Pasco and a couple of BioMarines. You'd best hustle. There's a lot of Martian activity out on the plain."

"Beating our feet," Archard said.

With him helping Katla support Captain Ferris, and Private Everett assisting Private Keller with Griffin, they made good time.

Archard expected the airfield to be hopping, with refugees from Bradbury showing up and the drop ships prepping for departure. He was mistaken. A lone ship sat in the middle of the field, its bay door down.

"All the other ships have left?" Katla said in dismay.

"They were probably full and couldn't wait," Archard guessed.

A pair of BioMarines, male and female, strode down the bay ramp. At sight of them, KLL-10 bounded ahead. She and the other female were happy to see each other.

Lieutenant Burroughs, in pilot's togs, came hurrying out to greet them, and snapped a salute. "I can't tell you how happy I am you made it. Five minutes more and I would have taken off."

"You're flying this thing?" Archard said.

"I'm a pilot, remember?"

"No, I mean where are the drop ship's pilot and co-pilot? Why you?"

"There was no one here when Private Pasco and I arrived. The bay was open but there was no sign of the crew. So I helped myself to a spare suit, and we're good to go."

"Thank God!" Katla exclaimed.

"We're not out of the woods yet," Lieutenant Burroughs said, and pointed. "There's a swarm of Martians heading our way."

53

The drop ship's hold consisted of a large bay for cargo and long rows of molded seats for troop transport up near the bulkhead to the bridge. Weapons lockers flanked the entry to the bridge with its array of controls as well as the pilot's and co-pilot's chairs.

Archard hurried everyone on board. He helped Katla strap Captain Ferris in, then strapped Katla in himself and went down the line ensuring everyone was secure.

Private Everett and Private Keller were in the last seats on either side.

"Good," Archard said, nodding. "Everyone is set to lift off."

"Except you and those critters, sir," the Kentuckian said with a nod.

Instead of claiming seats, the three BioMarines were holding onto straphangers and struts.

"You should strap in like the rest of us," Archard advised.

The hybrid called KLL-12 pointed. "Those seats were made for humans. We don't fit." He waggled the straphanger he was clutching. "We'll brace ourselves well enough."

"If you say so," Archard said dubiously.

"You're the one who should strap in, Captain," KLL-13 said. She grinned and winked. "We wouldn't want anything to happen to a handsome hunk of human like you."

"What?" Archard said, not sure he had heard right.

"Pay her no mind, Captain," KLL-12 said. "She doesn't have one."

"You made another funny!" KLL-13 squealed and batted her eyes at KLL-12.

He sighed.

Archard glanced at the pallets that filled the cargo area. Each bore a container the size of a small bus, standard for equipment and supplies sent from Earth. Stenciled on the nearest was *Hydroponic Units*.

Claiming an empty seat next to Private Everett, Archard strapped in and activated his commlink. "We're good to go, Lieutenant."

"None too soon, sir," she responded. "The Martians are closing fast."

"Then what are we waiting for?"

Over the intercom Burroughs blared, "Hang on, people! We're lifting hot!"

Normally, a drop ship rose slowly, then gradually accelerated to the delta-v needed to achieve orbit. Burroughs punched it straight off the landing pad. Their ship leaped into the air like a falcon taking wing, slamming them against their seats.

Archard heard Trisna and her daughter cry out. Private Griffin swore; hurt as he was, the G-Force compounded his pain.

Archard looked along the row at Katla and smiled encouragingly. She was holding Piotr's hand and smiled back. Lord, he couldn't wait for the two of them to reach Mother Earth and start their new life together.

"Goodbye Mars," Lieutenant Burroughs said over the speaker, "and good riddance."

"Amen to that," Private Everett said.

Archard's seat---in fact, the entire hold---was shaking like crazy. He had no fear of a hull breach. Drop ships were built to take the heaviest abuse that Nature, or an enemy, could dish out.

Some of the others didn't share his confidence. Trisna Sahir was as pale as the proverbial sheet. Behulah was quietly crying. Katla gripped her seat arms so tightly, her knuckles were white, while Piotr had closed his eyes and was silently mouthing a prayer.

Of all of them, the three BioMarines were taking it best. They stood straight and calm, KLL-12 staring at the cargo area with a peculiar expression on his reptilian features.

The shaking soon lessened and nearly everyone visibly relaxed.

Lieutenant Burroughs chose that moment to announce, "From here on out, it should be smooth going, people. We might run into a little chop, but that will be nothing. It will take us about ten minutes to achieve orbit. Over half the drop ships already have and will be docking with *Avenger I* and the rest of the space fleet.

Since we were last off, we'll be last to dock. I'll let you know which spaceship we're assigned to as soon as they tell me."

Archard didn't care which it was. The only thing that mattered now was reaching Earth safely and never, ever, setting foot off of it again. Wearily closing his eyes, he smiled to himself, thinking that not that many years ago, he couldn't wait to get off-planet. What a difference the destruction of three colonies made in his outlook.

"Captain Rahn?"

The voice was so close to Archard's ear, he sat bolt upright and grabbed for his sidearm.

KLL-12 was bending over him, legs braced, one hand on the top of Archard's seat. "Did I startle you, Captain? I apologize. I forget your senses are not as sharp as ours."

"What can I do for you?" Archard said more gruffly than he intended.

"I'm puzzled, Captain. Since you are the senior officer, I bring my puzzlement to you."

Archard refrained from remarking that the hybrid had a strange way of putting things. He settled for simply, "Oh?"

"I confess I'm not knowledgeable about all aspects of human affairs. I was created for war, after all, and that is my specialty."

"From what I've seen, the BioMarines are some of the best warriors anywhere," Archard said.

"We perform as required, don't we?" KLL-12 said.

"Beg your pardon?" Archard said.

KLL-12 gave the side of the hold a thump with his fist. "These drop ships are built for war too, are they not?"

"What else?" Archard said, uncertain where the hybrid was going with this.

"Whereas freighters are built for transporting freight, yes? Civilian freight, I mean?"

"Of course. So?" Archard said impatiently.

"So it puzzles me that we are transporting civilian freight into orbit," KLL-12 said.

"What?" Archard said, even though he knew what the hybrid was alluding to the moment the words were out of KLL-12's mouth. He glanced at the cargo area.

"Those containers, sir. They're supposedly filled with farming equipment. I realize human logic sometimes baffles me, but I can conceive of no reason for farming equipment to be on a drop ship. Perhaps you can enlighten me."

"I have no idea who put those containers on board," Archard said. "Or why."

"Ah. Then perhaps I should mention the other thing."

"What other thing?"

"I must have imagined it, sir."

"Damn it, what?"

"A few minutes ago, when we were shaking up a storm, as you humans would say, I could have sworn I heard something moving around."

"Moving around where?"

"What have we been talking about, sir?" KLL-12 said. He pointed at the nearest of the bus-sized containers. "I heard something moving around in there."

54

An awful feeling came over Archard. KLL-12 was absolutely right. There was no reason for military drop ships to be taking farm equipment into orbit. Which begged the question: how *did* the containers get there?

"Movement?" Archard rasped, his throat suddenly very dry.

"Yes, sir," KLL-12 said. "KLL-13 heard it, too. Very faint. Perhaps some of the equipment inside isn't properly secured."

Or maybe, Archard thought---and his mind rebelled at the image that sprang into his head.

"Sir? You appear upset."

Unbuckling his straps, Archard stood. He counted six containers, each large enough to contain hundreds of what common sense told him they couldn't possibly contain. "Can it be?"

"Captain?"

"Do you trust your ears?"

KLL-12 tilted his head. "Is that a trick question? Don't you trust yours?"

"What if the equipment hasn't broken loose?"

"Sir?"

"Could what you have heard be alive?"

"Alive?" KLL-12 repeated. He turned and stared at the containers. "What are you...?" He stopped, then said, "Oh."

"Oh is right," Archard said.

"Is what you are suggesting even possible?" KLL-12 said. "How would they have accomplished it?"

"If there's one thing I've learned," Archard said, "it's to never put anything past them."

Privates Everett and Keller had been listening and the Kentuckian said, "Past who, sir?"

"Who do you think? Stay put but keep your weapons ready." To KLL-12, Archard said, "Let's check it out."

They moved to the first container. KLL-12 put an ear to it and listened.

Boosting the audio input on his EVA suit to maximum, Archard did the same. Unfortunately, the background noise of the ship and the talking of the others drowned out any slight sounds that might come from the container.

"Hear any sounds?" Archard asked when KLL-12 stepped back.

"Nothing," the BioMarine said.

Archard walked around the container, looking for a hint of anything out of the ordinary. He went to the next, and a third. A few scratch marks caught his eye. They were recent, but could have been made when the forklift operator loaded the containers on board.

"Well, Captain?" KLL-12 said. "What do you think?"

"I don't know," Archard admitted.

"There's an easy way to find out, sir," KLL-12 said. "Let's open one."

"And if I'm right?" Archard said. "We can't fight a pitched battle in the hold." A stray shot would depressurize the ship, resulting in catastrophe.

"We could eject them."

"Not at this altitude."

The overhead speakers blared with another announcement by Lieutenant Burroughs, "Five minutes to orbit, people. We've been told to dock with the *John Carter*."

Archard had a decision to make, and fast. If his hunch was right, he didn't dare let the drop ship dock. He tried to tell himself he was being paranoid. After all, it would mean the Martians deliberately let some survivors reach the drop ships, counting on them, in their panic, to lift off without giving the containers a second thought. All so the Martians could reach the fleet. And then? Who knew?

"Captain?" KLL-12 said.

"We have to be sure," Archard said. "Check the weapons lockers. See how many flamethrowers we have on board."

A knowing smile spread across KLL-12's face and he moved off in long strides.

Archard keyed his commlink. "Lieutenant Burroughs, do you read me?"

"Affirmative, sir," she replied.

"Switch to O.F.," Archard directed, referring to the "Officer's Frequency," a private channel specifically for those in command. He did so, and said, "You there?"

"With ears open," Burroughs said.

"These containers in the hold. Do you have any idea how they got there?"

"No, sir. They were there when I reached the airfield."

"We might have hitchhikers."

"Sir?

"Listen to me, Lieutenant. I need you to get on the horn and contact the other drop ships. Find out if any of them have containers in their holds. If they do, advise them to maintain orbit and check the containers out before they dock."

"The admiral will want to know what is going on. He might not brook any delays."

"If he contacts you, tell him we're verifying if we have Martians on board."

There was a long pause, then Burroughs said quietly, "So that's what you meant about hitchhikers." She coughed. "Sir, you're not thinking of engaging them while we're in flight, are you? Surely you appreciate the risk involved."

"Would you rather they reach the fleet?" Archard said.

"Do you think they intend to destroy it?"

"That, or maybe something worse."

"What could be worse than..." Burroughs stopped. "Surely not? How would they accomplish it? They can't fly our spacecraft."

"If there's one thing I've learned in all this," Archard said, "it's to never take those things for granted. They've outsmarted us time and again."

"But to plan to invade Earth with our own spacecraft?"

"Why not? We invaded their world."

"God," Burroughs said. "Just when we thought we were safe."

"Keep your fingers crossed," Archard said.

"My toes, too," she said.

55

Archard was ready to find out if Schrodinger's cat was alive or dead.

Katla, Trisna, and the kids, as well as Captain Ferris and Private Griffin, both of whom were too hurt to be able to fight effectively, were on the bridge with Lieutenant Burroughs. The bulkhead had been sealed, and Burroughs was under orders not to open it under any circumstance until he gave the all-clear.

KLL-10 was with them. Her wound hadn't healed yet, so Archard told her to stay with the others. She didn't like it one bit.

Now, Archard stood at the front end of the first container, holding a flamethrower level at his waist, the tank heavy on his back. Beside him was Private Everett, similarly set to unleash liquid flame.

Off to one side, Private Keller had her ICW to her shoulder. So did young Private Pasco, a personable Spaniard who had been with Archard from the beginning at New Meridian.

"Remember," Archard said to the Kentuckian. "Confine your flame to the inside of the container."

"Easier said than done, sir," Everett said.

KLL-12 and KLL-13 stood to the other side, patiently waiting.

"Are you ready?" Archard said.

"I was born ready, Captain," KLL-13 said, and laughed.

KLL-12 nodded. "You can depend on us to do whatever is necessary."

"Then up you go," Archard said.

Tucking at the knees, KLL-12 and KLL-13 poised on the balls of their feet. Then, with deceptive and impressive ease, they leaped the full four meters onto the top of the container. Landing lightly, they moved to the front end and crouched.

"Sergeant Kline, you're up," Archard said. "Then get out of the way."

"You don't need to remind me twice, sir," the noncom said, coming around them to the control panel. "I don't intend to be fried to a crisp." He raised his fingers to the keypad. "Now?"

"Do it," Archard said.

Punching the code, Sergeant Kline skipped backward, raising his ICW as he did.

Archard heard the usual series of clicks and the hiss of the seal being broken that inevitably preceded the opening of a container door. The doors were designed to slide straight up. This one didn't. The hissing stopped and the door stayed closed.

"It must be jammed, sir," Sergeant Kline said.

"Try the panel again," Archard commanded. "Hit 'clear' first."

Once more the noncom sought to gain access. The light glowed green as it should and more clicks ensued, yet the door still refused to rise.

"What in hell?" Private Everett said.

"Maybe it's damaged," Private Pasco chimed in.

"Or someone doesn't want us to open it," KLL-12 said from his perch atop the container.

"Some*one*?" KLL-13 said. "Don't you mean some*thing*?"

Frustrated, Archard was tempted to give the door a kick. As fate would have it, his helmet crackled, causing him to turn partly away.

"Captain Rahn!" Lieutenant Burroughs said, sounding agitated. "I've talked to four of the other drop ships. They all report having containers in their holds similar to ours."

"Damn. Advise them to check the containers out, but to be careful."

"Will do."

"Captain!" Private Everett suddenly cried. "Lookout!"

The door was opening. Not slowly, as it should, but with lightning rapidity. In the blink of an eye it was all the way up--- and Martians spilled out in a living river of grippers and waving eye stalks.

Archard had no time to congratulate himself on being right. He opened up with his flamethrower, sending a jet of obliterating fire into the container's maw. So did Private Everett. Their combined chemical balefire charred the creatures in their tracks. But the deaths of those in front didn't deter those packed in behind them, and there were, as Archard had surmised, hundreds of the things, crammed into every centimeter of space. Some were burning, some were smoking, some were sizzling, yet out they came, scrabbling over the bodies of the fallen, using their blackened fellows as stepping-stones to get clear of the container.

"Open fire!" Sergeant Kline bawled, and he and Privates Keller and Pasco added a hailstorm to the fiery death dirge.

Still, Martians poured out. So far, only the crustoid crabs had appeared. But then, from the midst of the pack hurtled a blue warrior, smaller than most of its kind, probably so it wouldn't take up as much space in the container, but no less formidable.

Suddenly, the drop ship's hold had become a killing field.

"Back up!" Archard bawled at Everett, and they retreated in swift steps, their flamethrowers continuing to spew lethal tongues of orange and red.

Like a living battering ram, the blue warrior threw its massive bulk into the very heart of the flames, using its body to shield the rest.

KLL-12 and KLL-13 dropped onto Martian crabs scuttling wide to spread out and engaged then claws-to-grippers.

Pointing his nozzle at the blue warrior's sloping carapace, Archard poured on the fire, seeking to bring it down before it reached them. Everett was doing likewise, his flames splashing over the thing like sea water splashing over a boulder---but they had no effect.

Archard realized the warrior was going to reach them. A gripper, covered with sizzling fingers of fire, extended toward him, another toward the Kentuckian.

Faintly, over the din of their flamethrowers and the rattle of autofire, Archard heard the wail of the ship's alarms. Above them, the sprinklers activated, spraying a combination of water and fire-retardant in a downpour designed to put out any fire as quickly as possible.

Just as Archard's flamethrower went empty.

56

Archard braced for the worst. The blue Martian was almost on him and Private Everett.

But an incredible thing happened.

As the chemical rain fell on the Martians, they froze in place except for their eye stalks, which curved up toward the downpour. They stood as if transfixed, the fight seemingly forgotten.

Archard froze, too, momentarily baffled by their behavior. Then it hit him. According to the planetary scientists, it never rained on Mars. Or at least it hadn't in millennia. They attributed it to the low atmospheric pressure and low temperatures, and claimed that while it might snow now and again, the snow never reached the ground.

Which meant the Martians had never seen precipitation.

Never experienced rain or snow or sleet or hail. Never known a drizzle or a thunderstorm. To them, the chemical rain was a wonderment beyond their ken, or maybe something so sublime, it rendered them inert in fascination.

Whatever the reason, Archard seized the advantage. Flinging his flamethrower down and hurriedly discarding the tank, he unslung his ICW and bellowed, "Kill them! Kill them all!"

Everyone else had stopped firing, as astounded as Archard by the turn of events. Now they renewed their defense of the drop ship, with a vengeance. Lead poured into the Martians.

Archard and Everett concentrated on the blue warrior. The Kentuckian went so far as to run up to the creature and practically shove his muzzle into the thing's face. At that range, his armor-piercing rounds couldn't fail to penetrate.

Creatures dropped in heaps. The blue warrior lowered its eyes from the rain, staggered, and collapsed with a great flailing of its limbs and grippers.

Grabbing Private Everett by the scruff of his EVA suit, Archard hauled him backward before one of the flailing limbs struck him.

"We did it, sir!" Everett cried in elation. "We killed the critter!"

Archard gazed about the hold. The others were mopping up. KLL-12 and KLL-13, smeared all over in blood and bits, had cornered several crabs and were ripping them apart. He turned the other way, and stiffened.

Private Keller lay amid fallen monstrosities. She had been torn open from her navel to her neck, and her intestines had oozed out.

Private Pasco had been wounded in the leg but he was still on his feet and his suit appeared to be sealing.

Archard joined in the last of the slaughter. The Martians seemed sluggish. He wondered if it was the shock of their defeat, then decided, no, the chemical rain must have something to do with it. Unfortunately, the rain was ending. With the fire out, the ship's computer was shutting the system down.

Archard ordered the two BioMarines to rove among the dead creatures and make sure they were.

Sergeant Kline and Everett and Pasco came over.

"Looks like we did it, sir," the noncom said.

"We kicked butt," Everett said.

"Tell that to Private Keller," Archard said and turned toward the other containers on their pallets.

"Are there Martians in those, too?" Private Pasco said.

"Odds are," Archard said.

"Why didn't they help the others?" Sergeant Kline said.

"Your guess is as good as mine," Archard said.

His helmet crackled, and Lieutenant Burroughs practically shouted, "Captain! You need to get up here right away!"

Archard raised his left arm and waved it in a circle. "Listen up! Get to the bridge!" he shouted. "Everyone," he added when the BioMarines looked at him questioningly.

At the bulkhead, Archard pressed the comm button. "Open up, Lieutenant."

Katla was waiting just inside and embarrassed Archard a little by throwing her arms around him.

"Thank God you're alive."

"We're not done yet." Archard moved to the pilot's chair.

Burroughs was glued to her screens. The nightmarish spectacle they displayed explained why. "They both went up not seconds apart," she said.

Two of the drop ships had exploded. Coruscating clouds of debris were all that was left of their crews and refugees.

A speaker above the main console flared to life.

"This is Captain Sylvia Washington in drop ship M-23. Our ship has been overrun by Martians. We were examining the containers in our hold and out they came."

Archard was amazed at how calm she sounded.

"Everyone else is dead. I made it to the bridge and sealed the bulkhead but they are battering it down. It's only a matter of time."

Her tone took on a harder edge.

"I've pulled away from the fleet. As you can see on your screens, none of you are in danger of being collaterally damaged." She paused. "I'm about to self-destruct the M-23. I do this with a clear head and with full knowledge of the consequences. I can't let the Martians take control. There's no telling what they might do. They might be able to use my ship to ram the *Avenger I* or our other spacecraft. I can't allow that. Goodbye, one and all. This is Captain Sylvia Washington signing off. Booyah."

The explosion was spectacular.

Lieutenant Burroughs bowed her head, then swiveled her chair toward Archard. "What about us, sir? What do we do about those other containers?"

"I've been thinking about that," Archard said. "And I have an idea how we can dispose of them and maybe not get ourselves killed."

"That would be nice," Burroughs said.

57

Since drop ships weren't designed with comfort in mind, the bridge wasn't much bigger than a rec room at U.N.I.C. headquarters. Archard had Katla and Trisna and the children huddle around the chairs, and then the troopers huddled around them.

"As for you three," Archard said to the BioMarines, "I'd like you to lie flat against the bulkhead."

"To what end, Captain?" KLL-12 said.

"It's going to get bumpy," Archard said.

"I told you before," KLL-12 said. "We can handle a little bouncing around."

"Not this you can't. Lie down. That's an order."

Looking as he were lying down on a bed of putrid fungus, KLL-12 reluctantly obeyed.

KLL-13, laughing, slid down next, contriving to position herself so the upper part of her body was pressed against his. "Isn't this cozy?" she exclaimed with delight.

"I hate you," KLL-12 said.

KLL-10 eased down without complaint.

"Seal the bulkhead," Archard said to Burroughs.

She stabbed a button and a small screen lit with the words: SEAL ACTIVATED. "Done," she said. "But why? What in the world are you planning to do?"

"We're going to blow the containers into space."

Burroughs sat up so quickly, she almost bumped her head against his chin. "You want me to open the hold---in outer space? The decompression might rip us apart."

"We can't risk the Martians getting on board any of the spacecraft to Earth."

"But opening the hold?" Burroughs said. "It's not a trick they encourage us to try at the Academy."

Archard chuckled, then sobered. "If you have a safer means of doing them in, my ears are open. We used up the flamethrowers. And we certainly can't try grenades."

"But we're in space," Burroughs said almost breathlessly.

"Archard?" Katla spoke up. "How serious is this? The degree of danger?" She glanced apprehensively at Piotr and Behulah.

"Let me put it this way," Archard said. "If I had any other choice…"

"Oh," Katla said when he didn't go on.

Straightening, Archard surveyed the whole group. "Brace yourselves, people."

"Us too, sir?" KLL-13 said and giggled.

Archard leaned on the console and ran a forefinger along a row of controls until he came to the one he wanted. "Is this what I think it is?"

"It will unclamp the pallets the containers are strapped to," Lieutenant Burroughs confirmed. She indicated a large red button. "That's for the hold door. See the switch next to it? You have your choice of fast or slow."

"Slow would give them time to scramble out if they guess what we're up to."

"Fast it is, then, and may God help us," Lieutenant Burroughs said.

Archard looked around one last time. Katla was as grim as death. Private Everett and Captain Ferris nodded. KLL-13 waved.

"Do it, sir!" Private Everett said.

Archard pressed the release for the pallets, and on one of the screens the clamps attached to the bottoms of the containers popped off with loud clanks.

"Here we go," Archard said.

He pressed the red button. For the span of a single breath, nothing happened. Then the drop ship gave a violent lurch and the ship filled with the roar as of a thousand lions all at once. Behulah screamed.

There was a loud hiss, and metallic shrieking and grinding. Even though the bulkhead was sealed, Archard would swear some of the air was being sucked from the bridge.

He thought the worst was over, that it hadn't been as bad as he feared, but he was mistaken. The ship seemed to drop out from under them and then flipped back and forth.

Both Trisna and her daughter were screaming. Katla cried out. Several of the troopers swore and Private Griffin cried out in pain. KLL-13 laughed.

Struggling to hold onto the console, Archard saw Lieutenant Burroughs working to regain control. Before she could, the drop ship gave another spin and Sergeant Kline was thrown against the co-pilot's chair and fell.

On the screen, the containers were sliding toward the open bay door. As huge as they were, as heavy as they were, they were resisting the pull of the vacuum---but the void was relentless and slowly winning. Each container left drag marks on the floor.

Suddenly, one of them opened. The door slid high and out scrambled Martians, straight into the grasping maw of interstellar space. They were gone in a blink, whisked out and away with their limbs thrashing. Even a blue warrior was helpless in the grip of a fundamental force of nature.

Riveted to the screen, Archard was caught off-guard when the ship gave a brutal wrench. He crashed against the console, shoulder-first, forgetting his own plight. Another brutal wrenching of the ship reminded him. Burroughs had her hand poised near the red button but she held off pressing it.

One of the containers had been sucked into space but the other hadn't been expelled yet. It had spun around and a rear corner was wedged against the inner hull. Bucking and shaking, it tilted up at the other end. The door opened and desperate Martians bolted out, to be flung from the hold like so many leaves caught in a gale. Then, with an ear-blistering screech, the last container slipped loose and tumbled into the abyss.

Lieutenant Burroughs slammed the red button.

To Archard, it seemed to take forever for the bay door to close. The drop ship shook in spasms, like a sick patient, its gyros doing what they had been trying to do since the hold decompressed. Up became up and down became down, and the ship stabilized.

Moans and muttering filled the bridge.

Burroughs, her face caked with sweat, looked down at him and smiled. "We did it, sir."

"Booyah," Sergeant Kline said with a grimace.

Troopers echoed him.

Archard leaned on the console. "Sing out. Anyone badly hurt?"

"I stubbed a toe," KLL-13 said.

Archard grinned. She was something else. His grin faded, though, when he saw the wide-eyed expression of pure fear on Lieutenant Burroughs. "What?"

She pointed at the main view screen.

The *Avenger I* had pulled away from the fleet and was bearing down on them in full battle posture.

"What are they doing?" Burroughs said.

Archard grasped the significance even if she didn't. "Contact them! They're about to blast us to atoms!"

58

Burroughs anxiously nodded and flicked a switch and a speaker above the console blared to life.

"...is Admiral Thorndyke. If anyone on drop ship M-11 can hear me, respond immediately."

Pressing a tab, Burroughs said, "This is Lieutenant Ulla Burroughs on M-11. We can hear you, Admiral."

Thorndyke didn't acknowledge her transmission. Instead, the speaker blared, "I repeat. If anyone on drop ship M-11 can hear me, reply at once. Our sensors have picked up an ejection event on your ship. We have serious concerns you have been overrun by Martians."

"No!" Burroughs responded. "We are still in control!"

"If you do not respond," Admiral Thorndyke said. "I will have no recourse but to open fire."

"What's going on?" Captain Ferris said. "Why can't he hear us?"

"I don't know," Burroughs said while frenziedly flipping switches. "Maybe our communications have been damaged."

"If ship to ship doesn't work," Captain Ferris said, "try U.N.I.C.'s command frequency."

Archard should have thought of that himself. Quickly, he keyed in the numbers on the console and pressed his own mic. "This is Captain Archard Rahn on drop ship M-11. If you can hear me, Admiral, please acknowledge."

Tense seconds passed with everyone on the bridge glued to the speaker.

"I hear you, Captain," Admiral Thorndyke said. "A sitrep, if you please."

"We discovered Martians had snuck on board in cargo containers in our hold and ejected them," Archard said. "The ship is now clear of them and we are good to dock with the fleet."

"I'll be the judge of that," Admiral Thorndyke said. "Are you certain every last Martian is accounted for?"

"We believe so, yes, sir."

"Pressurize your hold and make absolutely certain," the admiral said. "I can't allow a single one of those things to reach the fleet."

"Understood, sir," Archard said.

"We've lost three drop ships," Admiral Thorndyke went on, "and two others besides yours report containers they can't account for. We've been discussing how to deal with them. Decompression was considered a last resort." He paused. "My compliments, Captain, on the fortitude it took. You could well have destroyed your ship."

"I'm all too aware of that, sir," Archard said, rubbing his shoulder.

"All right. Listen up. Once you have completed your search, you are to dock with the *Stanley*. Do you copy?"

"Yes, sir," Archard said. The *Stanley* was one of three cruisers, so-called because in size and armament they compared to the U.S. Navy cruisers of long ago.

"When you dock, no one is to leave your vessel until the *Stanley*'s crew has run a complete sweep of their own. Understood?"

"Yes, sir."

"Good. If you need me, contact me direct on this channel. Thorndyke out."

On the screen, the *Avenger I* veered away to resume its original position with the fleet.

"Pressurize the hold," Archard said to Burroughs.

"Already on it, sir."

Archard faced the rest. "You heard the man. As soon as it's safe, we spread out and search the hold from bottom to top. Every opening, every crack, every locker, every cabinet."

"There can't be any left, can there?" Katla said. "I mean, we all saw them being sucked out."

"I hope there isn't," Archard said. But he had to be realistic. It was entirely possible a few hadn't been expelled.

Private Everett patted his ICW. "Any still here will be right sorry they stayed, sir."

"I cannot wait to dock with the *Stanley*," Trisna Sahir said. "I will not feel safe until we do."

"I don't now as we'll ever be truly safe every again," Captain Ferris said.

Archard felt the same. The Martians had demonstrated a remarkable resiliency. They were able to survive in environments that would snuff humans like candles.

A large meter on the middle console showed the status of the pressurization, at the moment at forty-seven percent.

"It will take the pumps a bit longer," Archard said. "Relax until then."

"We could all take naps," Private Everett said, and KLL-13 cackled.

Glancing at her in annoyance, KLL-12 said, "I have a question, Captain."

"Which is?"

"What did the Martians hope to accomplish by sneaking those containers on board? To be taken to the fleet, obviously. What then? Destroy our spaceships in orbit?"

"Who can say?" Archard said.

"They have to know Earth would build more. That we would return."

"Maybe they wanted to send Earth a message. Leave us alone or else."

"Perhaps. But I can't help but think there is more to it."

"The hold is at sixty-one percent," Lieutenant Burroughs said.

"Troopers, check your weapons," Archard said. "BioMarines KLL-12 and KLL-13 will help with the hunt. KLL-10 will stay on the bridge and protect Lieutenant Burroughs and the wounded and the civilians."

"I'm missing all the action," KLL-10 said.

"Want me to bring you a Martian leg to gnaw on?" KLL-13 said.

"KLL-12 is right. You're weird," KLL-10 said.

"Booyah," KLL-13 said.

Archard turned to the screen that showed the hold. Debris lay everywhere. Cabinets and lockers had been torn open, their contents ripped into space. Nothing moved.

"Eighty-three percent," Burroughs said.

Katla placed her hand on Archard's arm. "Be careful in there."

"Goes without saying," Archard said.

"I would hate to lose you after all we've been through." She gently touched her faceplate to his in a tender display of affection.

"Sir, I have a question," Private Pasco piped up while slapping a magazine into his ICW.

"I'm listening," Archard said.

"The Martians. Those containers. When did they sneak them on board?"

"Probably during the attack on the colony," Archard speculated.

"Not after, though, right?"

"I don't see where that makes a difference."

"Don't you?" the young Spaniard said. "They had to find the containers. Then fill them with their, uh, people. Then other Martians had to carry the containers onto the drop ships and clamp them down and get out before they were seen. That took time. That took planning. It wasn't spur of the moment, sir."

"I agree. So?"

"So how much in advance did they plan all that? Did they attack Bradbury to keep us busy while they loaded the containers?"

"They've wanted our colonies destroyed from the beginning," Archard reminded him. But the Spaniard's question was troubling.

"Ninety-nine percent," Lieutenant Burroughs declared.

Archard hefted his ICW. "Up and at 'em, people. Time for some S and D."

"S and D?" Katla said.

"Search and destroy."

59

The bulkhead door slid open with a thunk.

Archard took point. His ICW pressed to his shoulder, he swung right and then left. "Clear," he said into his commlink.

"Sir, yes sir," KLL-13 said.

Archard suspected she was making fun of him but he let it pass. She did the same to everyone, to KLL-12 most of all. Shutting their dynamic from his mind, he said, "Everett, left. Pasco, right. Sergeant Kline, you have my back."

"What about us, sir?" KLL-13 wanted to know.

"Wait at the door until I yell for you."

"That's no fun," KLL-13 said. "Sir."

Archard became aware of a slight hiss from the direction of the hold door and wondered if the seal was compromised. He checked his holo readings. The pressure was holding, the air okay to breathe, which reminded him. "No one is to shed their EVA suit."

"Dang," Private Everett said. "Does this mean we can't prance around in our civvies?"

Sergeant Kline immediately jumped down his throat. "Clam up. Where do you think you are?"

Some of the lockers were still intact. Others, the doors had been ripped off or hung in strips. In several instances, the entire cabinet was twisted into so much scrap.

"We have to check these cabinets one by one," Archard told the others. "But first we sweep the hold." He moved between the rows of seats.

"There's not a speck of dust anywhere, sir," Private Pasco marveled.

"Pasco, what did I say about chatter?" Sergeant Kline said.

Archard crossed the length of the entire hold to the giant bay door. The hissing, he established, came from an inner seal that appeared to have been slightly crimped when the door closed. He wasn't overly worried the seal would give way. The synthetic compound used supposedly had the tensile strength of titanium.

Archard signaled to let his team know he was bearing right, and did so, roving his gaze over every square centimeter of floor and wall and ceiling. The Martians could be anywhere. The small red crabs, in particular, were able to contort and compress themselves into unbelievably small spaces.

"Sir!" Private Everett called out and motioned with the muzzle of his ICW.

A subsidiary control panel hung partway open. The lid could be opened by working a latch and swinging it up. The latch appeared to be broken off.

Archard signaled for the others to fan out. Once they had, he approached the panel, his finger curled around the trigger.

Using the tip of his flash suppressor, Archard edged the panel wider. The controls themselves were on a recessed pad. To tap them, you had to reach in. Below the pad was a fifteen-centimeter space between the cover and the wall.

Archard dipped his head to try and see down in.

Without warning, a Martian exploded out of the panel. A gripper speared at Archard's throat but snagged on the ICW's barrel. Throwing himself back, Archard tried to bring his weapon to bear but the creature clung to the barrel with one gripper while trying to rip him open with the other.

In his frantic haste, Archard tripped over his own feet and fell onto his back. He shoved at the thing with his weapon but couldn't knock it off. A gripper speared at his neck and missed.

Archard expected the creature's limbs to start ripping into him. Struggling to wrest his ICW free, he caught movement out of the corner of his eye. Suddenly, Sergeant Kline was there, shoving his ICW between the creature's eyes. He fired a three-round burst.

The Martian plopped onto Archard, limp as could be.

"Got it, sir," Sergeant Kline said. Stooping, he hauled the body off and sent it sliding along the floor, then offered his hand.

"You saved my hide," Archard said by way of gratitude.

"It's what we do," Kline said. "We're always there for a brother---or sister---in arms."

"Amen to that, Sarge," Private Everett said.

Archard collected himself. He ran a diagnostic on his EVA suit to confirm it hadn't been breached and signaled to move on. "Anyone sees any cracks, call out."

Damage caused by the decompression would be a perfect hiding place. So were shadowy sections of ceiling where lights had blown out.

"Nothing on my motion sensor, sir," Private Pasco said.

"Have you forgotten they're next to invisible?" Sergeant Kline said.

"I sure haven't," Everett said.

Neither had Archard. His EVA suit's full spectrum of sensors were next to useless.

His earphones chirped and Lieutenant Burroughs asked, "How is it going in there, sir?"

"We've only just started," Archard said. "Something up?"

"Another drop ship exploded. The captain piloting it was yelling something about Martians. They were close to the *Exeter*."

"The other cruiser? Was she damaged?"

"From the chatter I'm hearing, the damage is minimal. But Admiral Thorndyke is fit to be tied. He's issued an order that drop ships are not allowed near the fleet unless the drop ship has been confirmed cleared of Martians."

"He must know that's impossible," Archard said.

"Better not let the admiral hear you say that," Lieutenant Burroughs replied. "He might blow us to smithereens."

She was joking, but their exchange set Archard to contemplating a disturbing chain of thought.

60

Archard set the BioMarines to roving the hold. They leaped to the task like bloodhounds to the hunt. With their enhanced senses, it was Archard's hope that they could root out Martians that EVA suits' sensors might miss.

One thing Archard couldn't miss was a large jagged hole in the inner hull. Above it, the lights had blown out. Or did the Martians break them to cast that part of the hold in darkness?

Switching on his helmet's spotlight, Archard played the beam over the hole. It was about a meter across and half a meter high. Cautiously edging moving up to it, he bent his head to peer in.

Drop ships, like spaceships, were constructed in layers. There was the hull, then the cosmic ray barrier, then an interwoven network of baffles, filters, and structural supports, and finally the inner hull. Experience had shown that the double-hull system was remarkably effective at minimizing the chance of decompression.

The thing that bothered Archard was the realization that if the Martians penetrated the inner hull, the only way to find them would be to take the ship apart.

Thankfully, the hole wasn't deep. Several conduits had been exposed but they were intact. Archard craned his neck to try and see if there was enough space for a Martian to squeeze past the conduits but couldn't bend his head far enough.

"Clear, sir?" Private Pasco asked.

"Clear," Archard said, although he couldn't be entirely sure. Stepping back, he surveyed the whole expanse of the hold and inwardly shuddered.

"Something the matter, sir?" Sergeant Kline said.

"Just thinking," Archard said.

Private Pasco pointed. "Why is she flapping her arms like that?"

KLL-13 was in the pallet area, waving her arms back and forth and gesturing at the floor.

"She's found something," Private Everett stated the obvious.

Dreading what it would be, Archard led his men over.

KLL-12, seeing them converge, joined them.

"What have you got?" Archard said.

KLL-13 squatted and tapped a floor plate. "Notice anything, sir?"

Archard hunkered next to her. At first glance, no, he didn't. He shook his head.

"The angle, sir," KLL-13. "The gaps."

Archard stood and stepped back for a better view. The plate was two meters square. Unlike the other plates, which fitted snug one to the other, this particular plate had a thin gap around it. As if something had lifted it out and set it back in place but wasn't able to fit it exactly.

"And those," KLL-13 said, extending the tip of a claw at a specific spot.

Archard tensed. Scratch marks. As plain as anything. He motioned for his men to surround the plate. "Take either end," he said to KLL-12 and KLL-13. "On my mark, pry it out and tilt it but stay behind it in case they come out in a rush."

"There might be only one," KLL-13 said.

"One isn't enough to lift it," Archard said. The plates were heavy.

KLL-12 bent, inserted his claws, and slid his fingers under. "What are you waiting for, woman?"

"I didn't think you'd noticed," KLL-13 said, doing as he had done.

"On three," Archard said to them, crouching so he would be able to see under the plate as soon as it rose.

"One. Two. Three," he barked.

They raised the plate as he had instructed.

Nothing happened. Archard thought maybe they were wrong and leaned out.

A Martian burst from hiding.

Archard went to fire but the first was on him before he could. A gripper clamped onto his ICW, another snapped at his face. Jerking back, he saw that his muzzle was pointed right at the thing and fired. At that range, his ICW should have dropped it. But the Martian unexpectedly let go and scuttled toward the rows of seats--and the bridge.

"Stop it!" Archard bellowed.

Pasco triggered a burst but the creature was zigzagging to make itself harder to hit and none of his rounds scored.

Private Everett took deliberate aim and moved his muzzle back and forth, synchronizing his movements to those of his target. He fired on full auto.

Riddled, the Martian scrabbled another couple of meters and went limp.

Two more Martians burst out.

Archard dodged and rolled and came up shooting. He caught the closest broadside, stitching it from eye stalks to hind end. It sprawled in a jumble of legs and grippers, convulsed, and died.

Sergeant Kline was down on one knee. His suit was ripped high on his left arm and blood was dripping out. "Sorry, sir," he said. "The last one got past me."

"Where?" Archard said.

With his good arm, Sergeant Kline indicated a shadowed corner. "Somewhere there. I lost track of it."

"Get to the bridge. Have Dr. Dkany tend to you."

"I can manage," the noncom grunted, lifting his ICW.

"It wasn't a request."

KLL-13 nudged a dead Martian with her foot. "They aren't so much when there are only a few of them."

"One is all it takes, ma'am," Private Pasco said.

"It will take more than a single Martian to bring me down," KLL-12 declared.

"Humble fella, aren't you?" KLL-13 said.

"Back to work," Archard told them. "We have to find the third one. But first..." Moving to the exposed section under the plate, he checked for more. "There doesn't appear to be more."

"We were plumb lucky, sir," Private Everett remarked in his Southern drawl.

"How so?" Archard said.

"That plate wasn't over a maintenance crawl space," Everett said. "If it had been, the Martians could be anywhere on the ship."

Yet more cause for Archard to worry. Unfurling, he said, "Let's wrap this up so we can dock with the fleet."

"And then on to good old Mother Earth," Private Pasco said, and he and Private Everett and KLL-13 smiled.

Archard frowned.

61

The third Martian had fled into the darkest part of the hold.

That in itself was troubling. In all his encounters with the creatures, all the skirmishes and outright battles Archard had been in, not once had a Martian fled from a fight. Not once had he witnessed what he would describe as fear. Whatever else they might be, the Red Planet's denizens weren't cowards.

So the fact that this particular Martian had seen fit to run troubled Archard greatly. The creature must have an ulterior motive---and it wasn't hard for Archard to guess what the motive was. The things were determined to reach the fleet.

Signaling for the others to flank him, Archard maxed his sensors and stalked forward.

"Above you!" KLL-12 yelled.

Archard snapped his head back. "Where?"

"Unsure," the BioMarine answered. "I heard something. Scratching noises."

"Maybe it was a cockroach," KLL-13 said.

Archard was beginning to understand why KLL-12 became so annoyed with her. "Focus, all of you," he said. He swept the wall and ceiling with his motion sensor, but as usual, no targets.

"Sir!" Private Everett rang out. "To your left, about five meters up."

Archard looked but saw nothing. Increasing the magnification, he made out a bump about as big as his hand. Puzzled, he inverted the colors on his holo so that the wall blended into the background and the bump stood out. So did the appendages that radiated outward from the bump, and explained how the Martian was clinging to a flat surface almost as smooth as glass. "Good eyes, Private."

"Want me to do the honors, sir?"

"Go for it," Archard said.

The Kentuckian only needed a single burst to bring the creature crashing down. It landed on its carapace and kicked and flailed.

Walking up, Archard finished it off with rounds to the brain. As with Earth crabs, the Martian variety's cerebral center was between their eyes. Unlike their Earth cousins, dissection had revealed their brains were highly developed, in some respects even more so than humans.

"And that's that," KLL-13 said.

"Do we keep hunting, sir?" Private Pasco asked.

"We do," Archard confirmed.

They spent an hour at it and failed to turn up another otherworldly stowaway. Archard would have gone on searching indefinitely had his commlink not beeped.

"Captain Rahn," Lieutenant Burroughs said. "Admiral Thorndyke is on the line. He wants to know what is taking so long."

"Patch me through," Archard said.

Static sizzled, then, "Captain Rahn? This is the admiral. All the other drop ships have reported they are clean. What's the holdup at your end?"

"We were just completing our sweep," Archard told him.

"Any Martians left?"

"No, sir. But..."

"Good. You are cleared to dock with the *John Carter* and transship so we can get underway to Earth. I don't know about you, Captain, but I've seen enough of the Red Planet to last me a lifetime, and I didn't even set foot on it."

Archard realized his superior meant that to be humorous but he wasn't in the mood. "Sir, there's something I need to talk to you about..."

"Ring me up once you've docked."

"But, sir. It's important. I feel we---"

"After you've docked, Captain. Use a secure channel. Thorndyke out."

Static punctuated their conversation.

Archard returned to the bridge, every nerve in his body screaming that they were making a mistake,

Smiles of relief from everyone else greeted the news that they were finally able to hook up with the fleet. Trisna Sahir was so happy, she cried, which set her daughter to crying, too.

Katla picked up Piotr and hugged him. The troopers exchanged smacks on the shoulder, and thumbs-up. KLL-13 beamed and spread her arms toward KLL-12, who shook his head and wagged a finger at her. She laughed.

The docking was routine. As they emerged into the cruiser's enormous holding area, Archard was mollified, somewhat, to find a squad of troopers waiting. They had been sent to stand guard over the drop ship. The sergeant in charge told Archard that special TAC teams were going through all the drop ships to make sure every Martian was accounted for.

An ensign ushered them to their quarters. Archard was given a berth in the officer's wing. No sooner did the ensign close the door behind her than he was on the horn to the admiral. He figured he might have to wait, but no.

Thorndyke filled the screen. He appeared tired and worn, and rubbed his eyes. "Captain Rahn. You didn't waste any time."

"You know why I'm calling," Archard guessed.

"I do," Admiral Thorndyke said.

"I'd like to go on record as opposing our return to Earth."

"Give me an alternative, Captain."

"Sir?"

"We can't stay in orbit forever. Eventually, we'll run out of supplies. What other options do we have? We can try to retake Bradbury but we both know how that will go. We could land somewhere else but the Martians are bound to find us eventually. Or we could strike off into deep space and hope to find a habitable planet. The odds are about the same as winning the lottery."

"Our prospects are bleak, I grant you," Archard said.

"I'm going to ask you a question, Captain," the admiral said. "Answer honestly."

"Always, sir."

"You have more experience with the Martians than anyone alive," Thorndyke said. "Based on that experience, what would you say the odds are that a few Martians are still alive on some of the drop ships?"

"Ninety-nine-point-nine percent."

"That's what I was afraid of," Admiral Thorndyke said, despondently. "But it doesn't make a difference."

"It most surely does, sir!" Archard disagreed. "We can't take those things back to Earth, no matter how few there are. There's no telling what will happen. If they find a way to multiply..." He didn't finish. There was no need.

"You think I'm not aware of the risk?" Admiral Thorndyke grew more haggard right before Archard's eyes. "I'm also responsible for the lives of over two thousand personnel. And I refuse to consign them to certain death. Which is how all those other scenarios would end. And you know it."

"We're talking two thousand against the lives of everyone on Earth," Archard said.

"You don't know that. Not beyond any shadow of a doubt. Don't claim that you do."

Archard stayed silent.

"I've been in contact with the secretary-general and he agrees," Admiral Thorndyke said. "We'll return to Earth, place the ships under quarantine, and hope for the best."

"Damn," Archard said.

"I know. Sometimes we have to roll the dice whether we want to or not. Thorndyke out."

The screen went blank.

Archard switched it off and sat back. He was suddenly bone-tired. He was about to lie on his bunk when his door chirped. Rising, he opened it, and Katla was in his arms, her lips on his.

"Here you are! Trisna and I are on the next level up. She's watching Piotr to give us some time alone." Katla smiled and rubbed the tip of her nose against his. "I could use a shower? How about you?"

Despite himself, Archard smiled. "I suspect you're trying to seduce me, madam."

"Oh really, Sherlock?" Katla laughed and kissed his cheek. "Are you as excited as I am to put all this behind us? To be safe once again?"

Captain Archard Rahn listened to the thrum of the spaceship's engines and gazed out the porthole at the world that the ancient Greeks had called Ares, after their god of war, and the later Romans then called Mars, after their own war god. The Chinese named it the Fire Star and said it was a harbinger of grief and war.

Subsequent generations came to refer to it simply as the Red Planet. Fitting names, he reflected, one and all.

"Think of it!" Katla exclaimed. "To live out the rest of our lives without ever setting eyes on another Martian. How great is that?"

"One can only hope," Archard said.

FINI

CHECK OUT OTHER GREAT SCIENCE FICTION BOOKS

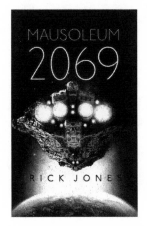

MAUSOLEUM 2069
by Rick Jones

Political dignitaries including the President of the Federation gather for a ceremony onboard Mausoleum 2069. But when a cloud of interstellar dust passes through the galaxy and eclipses Earth, the tenants within the walls of Mausoleum 2069 are reborn and the undead begin to rise. As the struggle between life and death onboard the mausoleum develops, Eriq Wyman, a one-time member of a Special ops team called the Force Elite, is given the task to lead the President to the safety of Earth. But is Earth like Mausoleum 2069? A landscape of the living dead? Has the war of the Apocalypse finally begun? With so many questions there is only one certainty: in space there is nowhere to run and nowhere to hide.

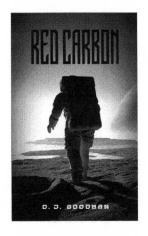

RED CARBON
by D.J. Goodman

Diamonds have been discovered on Mars.

After years of neglect to space programs around the world, a ruthless corporation has made it to the Red Planet first, establishing their own mining operation with its own rules and laws, its own class system, and little oversight from Earth. Conditions are harsh, but its people have learned how to make the Martian colony home.

But something has gone catastrophically wrong on Earth. As the colony leaders try to cover it up, hacker Leah Hartnup is getting suspicious. Her boundless curiosity will lead her to a horrifying truth: they are cut off, possibly forever. There are no more supplies coming. There will be no more support. There is no more mission to accomplish. All that's left is one goal: survival.

CHECK OUT OTHER GREAT SCIENCE FICTION BOOKS

IN PERPETUITY
by Jake Bible

For two thousand years, Earth and her many colonies across the galaxy have fought against the Estelian menace. Having faced overwhelming losses, the CSC has instituted the largest military draft ever, conscripting millions into the battle against the aliens. Major Bartram North has been tasked with the unenviable task of coordinating the military education of hundreds of thousands of recruits and turning them into troops ready to fight and die for the cause.

As Major North struggles to maintain a training pace that the CSC insists upon, he realizes something isn't right on the Perpetuity. But before he can investigate, the station dissolves into madness brought on by the physical booster known as pharma. Unfortunately for Major North, that is not the only nightmare he faces- an armada of Estelian warships is on the edge of the solar system and headed right for Earth!

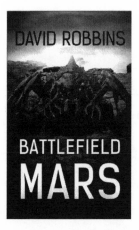

BATTLEFIELD MARS
by David Robbins

Several centuries into the future, Earth has established three colonies on Mars. No indigenous life has been discovered, and humankind looks forward to making the Red Planet their own.

Then 'something' emerges out of a long-extinct volcano and doesn't like what the humans are doing.

Captain Archard Rahn, United Nations Interplanetary Corps, tries to stem the rising tide of slaughter. But the Martians are more than they seem, and it isn't long before Mars erupts in all-out war.

CHECK OUT OTHER GREAT SCIENCE FICTION BOOKS

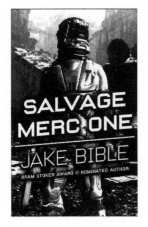

SALVAGE MERC ONE
by Jake Bible

Joseph Laribeau was born to be a Marine in the Galactic Fleet. He was born to fight the alien enemies known as the Skrang Alliance and travel the galaxy doing his duty as a Marine Sergeant. But when the War ended and Joe found himself medically discharged, the best job ever was over and he never thought he'd find his way again.

Then a beautiful alien walked into his life and offered him a chance at something even greater than the Fleet, a chance to serve with the Salvage Merc Corp.

Now known as Salvage Merc One Eighty-Four, Joe Laribeau is given the ultimate assignment by the SMC bosses. To his surprise it is neither a military nor a corporate salvage. Rather, Joe has to risk his life for one of his own. He has to find and bring back the legend that started the Corp.

SERENGETI
by J.B. Rockwell

It was supposed to be an easy job: find the Dark Star Revolution Starships, destroy them, and go home. But a booby-trapped vessel decimates the Meridian Alliance fleet, leaving Serengeti—a Valkyrie class warship with a sentient AI brain—on her own; wrecked and abandoned in an empty expanse of space. On the edge of total failure, Serengeti thinks only of her crew. She herds the survivors into a lifeboat, intending to sling them into space. But the escape pod sticks in her belly, locking the cryogenically frozen crew inside.

Then a scavenger ship arrives to pick Serengeti's bones clean. Her engines dead, her guns long silenced, Serengeti and her last two robots must find a way to fight the scavengers off and save the crew trapped inside her.

Made in the USA
Middletown, DE
20 July 2021

44476721R00125